"Are you always this relentless?"

"On occasion I've been considered determined," Shane admitted. "I just feel bad about what happened."

"Well, don't. It won't change anything." She hopped out of the SUV and leaned back in when Shane and Jason stayed put. "Are you two coming in?"

"In a while. We'll walk around here first. Visit the playground."

Whitney grinned at the child and walked toward the main entrance. Once there, she peered back at the SUV. She glimpsed Shane's attention directed at her, and a shiver of awareness shimmied down her back. He was an attractive man, but their worlds were vastly different. She'd promised herself she was going to start over, make something of herself. Finally get her plans in place. And they certainly didn't include getting involved with a man. Especially not Shane…

Books by Margaret Daley

Love Inspired

The Power of Love
Family for Keeps
Sadie's Hero
The Courage to Dream
What the Heart Knows
A Family for Tory
*Gold in the Fire
*A Mother for Cindy
*Light in the Storm
The Cinderella Plan
*When Dreams Come True
*Tidings of Joy
**Once Upon a Family
**Heart of the Family
**Family Ever After
**Second Chance Family

*The Ladies of Sweetwater Lake
**Fostered by Love

Love Inspired Suspense

Hearts on the Line
Heart of the Amazon
So Dark the Night
Vanished
Buried Secrets
Don't Look Back
Forsaken Canyon
What Sarah Saw
Poisoned Secrets

MARGARET DALEY

feels she has been blessed. She has been married more than thirty years to her husband, Mike, whom she met in college. He is a terrific support and her best friend. They have one son, Shaun. Margaret has been writing for many years and loves to tell a story. When she was a little girl, she would play with her dolls and make up stories about their lives. Now she writes these stories down. She especially enjoys weaving stories about families and how faith in God can sustain a person when things get tough. When she isn't writing, she is fortunate to be a teacher for students with special needs. Margaret has taught for over twenty years and loves working with her students. She has also been a Special Olympics coach and participated in many sports with her students.

Second Chance Family
Margaret Daley

**Steeple
Hill®**

Published by Steeple Hill Books™

STEEPLE HILL BOOKS

Steeple
Hill®

Recycling programs
for this product may
not exist in your area.

ISBN-13: 978-0-373-81413-8

SECOND CHANCE FAMILY

Copyright © 2009 by Margaret Daley

For if ye forgive men their trespasses, your
heavenly Father will also forgive you:
But if ye forgive not men their trespasses,
neither will your Father forgive your trespasses.
—*Matthew* 6:14–15

To my husband, Mike, who I love dearly

Chapter One

"This is not negotiable. My son *will* attend your school, starting this Thursday." After dealing with a suicidal teenage girl most of the night, Dr. Shane McCoy didn't need this.

"We aren't equipped to deal with him. Jason should go to Eisenhower Elementary where there's a class for children like him," the principal said in a tight, highly controlled voice.

The woman's last sentence shredded what composure he had. Pacing his bedroom, Shane plowed his fingers through his hair and tried to remain calm. He gripped the phone. "You've known he would attend for months."

The rumble of thunder in the distance drew him toward an upstairs window at the front of his house. Jason didn't do well in thunderstorms. *Please, Lord, don't let it rain—not today.* He drew back the drapes and searched the sky. Dark clouds raced toward the east, away from his house.

"We've tried to find the right staff to handle your son, but…" The woman paused, taking a deep breath.

Jason appeared on the sidewalk leading from his house. What was he doing out front? Going to get the newspaper for Aunt Louise?

"But there aren't—" the woman continued on the other line.

When his son ignored the paper lying in the grass, concern shot through Shane. He hurried toward his door. "I'll be there for the meeting this afternoon. I've got to go," he said, and clicked off the cell phone.

Am I making a mistake?

As the question intruded into Whitney Maxwell's mind, her long hair whipped across her face, momentarily obstructing her view of the street she drove down.

"Jason! Stop!"

To the right of her someone's frantic tone pierced the early morning air. Whitney fought the wayward strand, finally managing to hook it behind her ear at the same time her gaze riveted to a sudden movement. A child disappeared between two parked vehicles ahead of her, a second later reappearing in the path of her car as he raced across the road.

Clenching the steering wheel of her convertible Volkswagen vehicle, she jerked to full attention and slammed on the brakes. Not soon enough.

Without thought Whitney swerved her VW to the right. Into a big SUV. The sound of crunching metal drowned out the thundering of her heartbeat in her ears. When she was thrown forward, her seat belt halted her progress. The strap cut into her chest, disrupting her shallow breaths.

Almost to the other side of the street near a yellow trash can, the little boy stopped, pivoted and came straight toward her. When he reached the crash, he slid his hand over the smashed hood of her car, his gaze glued to it.

"Jason! Jason!" the woman screamed, her view blocked by the big SUV.

The little boy looked up, cocked his head, then whirled around and ran back the way he came— straight into the arms of the older woman who rushed between the parked vehicles. Whitney stared into the lady's pale face as she quaked and hugged the child to her.

Everything happened so fast—only seconds— that Whitney's head spun. Her hands shaking, she fumbled for the handle. She shoved the door open, swung her legs to the pavement and stood.

The thought of the near miss shuddered through her. Her legs weak, she started to sink and clutched the car to steady herself. She needed to check on the little boy and the older woman, but her whole body quaked. Drawing in several stabilizing breaths, she made her way to the pair now on the grass between the sidewalk and the street.

The older woman, tears in her eyes, held the child away from her. "Jason, you *cannot* run out into the street."

"Like yellow."

Yellow? What's the child talking about?

"Wanted to touch. So pretty."

Whitney glanced toward the trash can then at her yellow Volkswagen car. Her steps faltered at the implication of what could have happened. Thankfully she'd only been going twenty-five miles per hour because the child had been oblivious to the danger involved, and yet he appeared to be at least six or seven years old.

The sounds of a slamming door and pounding footsteps nearby drew Whitney's focus toward the house in front of her. A large man, over six feet tall, jogged across the lawn toward them. His intense gaze first took in the child and woman, then slipped to Whitney hovering a few feet from the pair. It skimmed down her length before moving away. When his appraisal connected with her Volkswagen bug, a frown carved hard lines into his face.

"Aunt Louise, what happened?"

"Jason—" the older woman whimpered the name, tears streaking down her face as she clung to the child. "He—he…"

After patting the woman and whispering, "It's okay. I'll deal with this," the man fixed his gaze on Whitney and strode toward her. "What happened?"

His question frosted the air between them. She straightened, her hands clenched at her sides. "The little boy ran out into the street from between these two parked cars." She gestured toward the vehicles. "I had to swerve to avoid hitting him."

His color drained from his face. He glanced over his shoulder at the boy and the older woman. The child tried to pull from her embrace, his arm outstretched toward Whitney's VW.

"Aunt Louise, can you take Jason inside? I'll be there in a minute." When the pair was on the porch, the man turned back to Whitney. "I'm so sorry. Are you okay?" His cultured voice held a smooth, calmer tone, meant to put a person at ease. Concern—directed totally toward her— darkened his green eyes.

"Better than my car." She flipped her quivering hand toward her convertible. "I ran into someone's SUV. I—"

"Don't worry about that. It's mine. Cars can be fixed much easier than people." He walked toward the back of his vehicle and examined the damage. When he looked at hers, he whistled. "Yours will be more involved."

"Yeah. It's sorta like a beetle slamming into a wall." Where was she going to get the money to pay for this? Even if the man could take care of his SUV, her car repairs would cost a lot and with a five-hundred-dollar deductible— money she didn't have—she had no answer. She would not accept any more help from her older brother. She'd always managed to make her way in the world by herself. She wasn't going to let this change that. She would figure out something.

After rounding the back of her vehicle and inspecting the crash from all angles, the man came back to her side. "I see what you mean. I'll take care of your car."

"No, I crashed into your SUV."

"But if you hadn't reacted quickly, my son would have been hit. I owe you. I'll take care of it." He stuck his hand out for her to shake. "Shane McCoy."

"I'm Whitney Maxwell." His warm, firm clasp conveyed a man who took charge of situations and solved problems. Her defenses quickly went up.

"Noah's sister?"

"Yes, you know my brother?"

"I've been working with Stone's Refuge ever since it began. And since he's on its board, we've gotten to know each other these past few years."

Now that she was thinking somewhat rationally, she remembered Noah talking about a Dr. McCoy seeing some of the kids who lived at Stone's Refuge, a place for foster children who needed help. "You're the child psychologist." Then she recalled her brother mentioning how much Dr. McCoy had helped his adopted son. "The one who worked with Rusty."

"Your brother was the best thing that happened to Rusty."

"I think my nephew would agree. Noah's taken to being a dad." Although she had discovered she loved children since returning to Cimarron City, she never saw herself as a mother. She never wanted to disappoint a child like she had been.

"Come in and I'll call a wrecker to take your car to a shop I know that does excellent work for a fair price."

Shane McCoy had everything figured out. She fortified her defenses. "I'll drive my car to school and come up with something."

He shook his head. "That car isn't going anywhere without a wrecker."

Whitney did her own examination of her VW and noticed the front hood was crumpled into her right tire. He was correct. Although the school was about two miles away, maybe she could walk and still make it on time. She glanced down at her watch and winced. That wasn't an option if she wanted to be on time or at least only a few minutes late.

"You mentioned driving to school—the university?"

"No, Will Rogers Elementary School."

"You're a teacher there?"

"A teacher's assistant." If all her plans worked out, she would be a teacher in three years.

"My son starts kindergarten there on Thursday. We've been marking off the days until school starts. So since I was going there this morning anyway to show Jason around before the meeting there this afternoon, I can take you. That's the least I can do."

She looked down at the damaged hood. "Fine, but I need to call a wrecker then the school to let them know I'll be a few minutes late." She hated being late her first day on the job, but there was just so much help she would accept from Shane McCoy.

"Are you sure I can't arrange for a wrecker to take your car to Carl's Body Shop?"

"I'm sure." If she had been paying better attention instead of looking for Zoey Crandell's house, maybe she would have seen the child racing across the lawn toward the street. But ever since she'd made the decision to move out of her brother's guesthouse, her attention had been focused on finding an apartment, and Zoey's sounded perfect for her.

"You can call inside while I prepare Jason to leave now."

"Prepare?" slipped out before Whitney could stop it. Jason didn't act like a normal kindergartner. What was wrong with him?

"It won't take long. I just have to prepare my son for something a little different. He already knew he was going to the school today." Shane started for the large Victorian house, stopped and said, "My aunt makes a great cup of coffee. Would you like some?"

"That sounds good." Whitney reached into her VW and grabbed her purse and the classified section of the newspaper she'd brought with her. Peering at a circled ad, she noted the address she'd been searching for and the reason she was on this particular street. "Do you know Zoey Crandell?" she called out to Shane.

He paused a few steps away from her and swung back around. "Yes, she lives at the end of this block." He pointed toward another Victorian house five away from his on the other side of the street.

Whitney noticed he wore a wedding ring and wondered where his wife was since it wasn't much after seven. "I wanted to get a peek at the garage apartment she had advertised for rent," she said when she saw the question in his eyes.

"That's right. She does rent that out. I didn't realize her tenant left."

"Have you ever seen it?"

"No, but she's a good neighbor. She goes to my church." Shane started again for his front door.

As Whitney ambled toward the house, she thought about the little boy she'd almost hit. Her earlier question crept again into her mind. Was she making a mistake? Maybe her wanting to be a teacher wasn't what she should do with her life. Before coming back to Cimarron City nine months ago, she would never have dreamed of becoming a teacher and not all children were like her niece and nephews. Ones like Jason would be a challenge. Could she deal with that?

She couldn't get the image out of her mind of the child coming out between the parked vehicles so suddenly, then after she had crashed, walking over to her car and touching it. In her education classes she took at night at the university, she hadn't had the Exceptional Child course yet, but it was obvious something wasn't right with Shane McCoy's son.

But wasn't that why she had decided to be a teacher's assistant? To see if she could handle sthe job?

Inside his house Shane immediately headed toward the kitchen, which flowed into a den. Whitney followed. His son sat cross-legged on the floor in front of the television, watching Animal Planet and rocking back and forth, while he clutched a yellow cloth.

"Aunt Louise, this is Whitney Maxwell, Noah's sister. I'm going to drive her to Will Rogers Elementary School where she works."

His aunt smiled at Whitney then turned to Shane and said, "Are you taking Jason?"

"Yeah, since later this afternoon I have that meeting at the school and I don't know how long it will last." He handed Whitney a cordless phone and the telephone book.

While she placed a call to a wrecker service and the school, he poured coffee into a mug sitting on the counter then took a new one down from a cabinet and filled it for Whitney. He handed it to her as she wrapped up her second call.

After taking a large sip of the brew, Shane strode toward the den area and knelt next to his son. He placed his hand on the boy's arm before he said his name. Pressing a yellow cloth to his chest, Jason slowly looked up at his dad. Shane's lowered voice didn't carry to Whitney.

"He has the patience of Job."

Surprised by the comment, Whitney turned on

her heel and faced the older woman, slim, medium height, her gray hair pulled back in a bun at the base of her head. "Shane?" She picked up her mug and drew in a deep breath of the coffee-laced air.

"Yes. It's been hard since his wife died."

"Oh, she died recently?" Whitney asked, remembering the ring on his hand.

"Five years ago so he's been mostly the one responsible for raising Jason. He does a wonderful job with his son. If anyone can prepare Jason for a change, it's my nephew."

What happens if you don't prepare Jason? Whitney wanted to ask the question, but it was a private affair, and if anyone understood the need for privacy, it was she. That thought prompted a decision to call Zoey Crandell and set up an appointment this week to see the apartment because at Noah's estate—as large as it was—she never had much alone time.

Louise released a deep sigh. When she brushed back a stray strand of hair, her hand shook. "I'm not nearly as good as Shane, hence the runaway this morning. Jason didn't like the breakfast I fixed him. We'd run out of his favorite cereal so I made him pancakes, his second favorite. I don't move as fast as I once did. He was out the front door before I could stop him. I'm so sorry for what happened. Are you all right?"

The concern in the woman's brown eyes reflected the same concern as her nephew's earlier. Although her chest hurt where the strap wrenched her to a stop, she wouldn't add to this woman's worry. "I'm fine," she hurriedly said to reassure Louise who was still visibly upset even if she was trying to present a calm front.

"I'm so glad of that. Thankfully Jason's favorite program was on, and he didn't object to coming back inside. That gave me some time to settle my nerves."

"I understand he's starting kindergarten on Thursday at the school where I work." Whitney took a swig of coffee, its taste smooth and rich like Shane's voice.

Louise's eyebrows crunched together. "Before this year, he went to a private special school, but Shane feels he needs more exposure with regular children. I'm not sure that's a good idea."

"What's wrong with Jason?" The second she asked the question she wanted to take it back. It wasn't her business, and she normally stayed out of others' affairs and problems. She had enough of her own to deal with.

"He's autistic."

Whitney's gaze flew back to the pair on the floor in front of the television. She didn't know much about autism, but she knew it could be very challenging for teachers and parents. Again the niggling doubt surfaced.

"We're ready to go. When is the wrecker going to be here?" Shane asked as he approached her.

"Half an hour. I've given the man all the information. If I leave, will my car be okay until the wrecker comes?"

Aunt Louise stepped forward. "I'll keep an eye out for the wrecker. This street doesn't have much traffic." She splayed her hand over her heart. "I thank the Lord every day for that fact. Don't worry about your car. It's off to the side, and if someone wants to get by, they can."

Whitney nodded. "Thanks." She was already late for her first day and didn't want to make it worse.

Jason stood behind his father, and when he glanced up and *really* saw her, he flew at Whitney. Surprised, she stepped back.

The boy opened and closed his hand as though he wanted something. "Yellow hair. Touch."

"Jason, you can't—"

"That's okay," Whitney said, interrupting Shane.

She knelt in front of the child and smiled. He didn't look at her face but fixed upon her hair, stroking its long strands over and over.

"Pretty."

Whitney caught sight of Shane hovering close

beside his son. Worry had returned to his expression, his eyebrows coming together, lines wrinkling his forehead. She started to rise when the child grabbed a fistful of her hair but didn't pull it.

Shane shifted forward to intervene. "Sorry. His favorite color right now is yellow." He touched his son's shoulder and moved to where he was in the boy's line of vision. "Jason, are you ready to go for a ride? You can touch the yellow car one more time before we leave to go to school. But this time you will have to walk with me in order to touch the car. You are never to run in the street by yourself."

"Yellow car."

"But first, Jason, you need to let go of Whitney's hair."

"Touch yellow car." The child released his grip and her strands fell back into place.

Whitney quickly rose while Jason took his father's hand, tugging him toward the front door.

Shane threw a sheepish look at her. "I guess he's ready to go."

After Jason took a few moments to pat and stroke her yellow car, she found herself sitting in the front seat of the SUV while Shane buckled his son in the back one. Jason rubbed a yellow cloth between his forefinger and thumb and stared at the floor. He seemed unaware of what his father was doing.

Shane switched on the engine and peered at her. "I want to at least pay for the damages to your car."

"My insurance will take care of it."

"Not your deductible. I'll take care of that. How much is it?"

Whitney hesitated. She wasn't quite sure how to take Shane. She realized she'd veered to avoid hitting his son, but she had crashed into his SUV.

"Please, Whitney. The situation could have been so much worse if you…" He snapped his mouth closed, a nerve twitching in his jaw. "Let's just say I'm grateful you're a quick thinker."

"Five hundred dollars."

He blew out a long breath, throwing his SUV into Drive and pulling away from the curb. "Thanks. I appreciate you letting me do this." He slanted her a look. "I'll also pay for a car rental. You can't go without a means of transportation."

She hadn't even thought about that. Shane had a way of covering all the bases, which made her squeeze her hands together in her lap. "I'll take care of it." Embedding strength into each word, she was determined to make it clear she didn't like accepting help like he was throwing at her. She didn't want to be beholden to anyone, and she already had allowed her older brother to do too much for her. That had to end.

Thankfully he must have gotten the message because he didn't say anything else. She relaxed back and uncurled her hands.

When they passed Zoey Crandell's house, she looked down the driveway at the two-car garage with an apartment over it. The well-groomed yard with neatly tended flowerbeds and two maples standing sentinel out front appealed to Whitney. She peered back at the quiet street, shaded with large trees. She liked the area.

Ten minutes later, Shane parked in the oval lot in the center of the elementary school campus. "Are you sure I can't do anything else?"

"Yes," she said, then shook her head. "Are you always this relentless?"

"On occasion I've been considered determined. I just feel bad about what happened."

"Well, don't. It won't change anything." She hopped out of the SUV and leaned back in when Shane and Jason stayed put. "Are you two coming in?"

"In a while. We'll walk around out here first. Visit the playground."

Whitney grinned at the child. "Jason, I'll see you later."

The little boy ignored her and continued to rub his cloth, his gaze fastened onto the back of the seat in front of him.

After a half minute of silence, she swept her glance to Shane. "Thanks for the ride."

"Let me know when you need the money for the deductible."

"Sure. I'll know more after I talk with my insurance agent and the body shop." Quickly she shut the car door and hurried toward the primary building.

At the main entrance she peered back at the SUV. She glimpsed Shane's attention directed at her, and a shiver of awareness shimmied down her length. He was an attractive man, but their worlds were vastly different. Besides, when she'd come back to Cimarron City nine months ago, she had promised herself she was going to start over, make something out of herself. Finally her plans were in place. And they certainly didn't include getting involved with a man.

Chapter Two

"Thanks for showing me the ropes around here, Amanda." Whitney stood and stretched her muscles, which had cramped from her sitting on the floor while she labeled cubicles and supplies. Sweat beaded her forehead and upper lip. "I hope they can get the air-conditioning fixed by the time school starts in a few days."

"I was hoping it would rain today and cool things off, but it passed us by." Dressed in a turtleneck shirt and jeans, Amanda Miller, another teacher's assistant, gathered up the labeling machine and markers they used.

"I can imagine. I would have roasted in what you're wearing." Thankful she had on a split skirt and a short-sleeve blouse, Whitney didn't know why the young woman hadn't gone home at lunch and changed. Whitney knew from their conversation earlier that Amanda only lived a few blocks away from the school with her boyfriend.

"I'm always cold," Amanda said, but her armpits were drenched with perspiration. Still sitting, she turned away to put the pens in a box.

"Oh, there's…" Whitney reached toward Amanda to snatch up a marker on the floor next to the young woman that Whitney had missed while cleaning up.

The redhead flinched when she shifted back around and glimpsed Whitney out of the corner of her eye. She grabbed the black pen and gave it to Amanda. The woman's hand quivered as she took the marker.

Strange, Whitney thought. She'd remembered right before lunch, when another teacher's assistant had popped into the room they were working in, her sudden appearance had startled Amanda and she'd shaken even more right after that.

"I'm glad it's time to leave. All I'd like to do is soak in a hot tub, but when I get home, I have too much to do." Whitney put the labeling machine on the teacher's desk. "How about you?"

"Yeah, I still have housework to do and to fix dinner." Amanda pushed to her feet.

"A frozen meal is about all the energy I have to make tonight. See you tomorrow."

Exhausted after her first day on the job of

meetings and helping prepare the classroom for the children, Whitney gathered her purse, then headed toward the front doors. Coming around the corner, she nearly collided with Shane leaving an office near the main entrance. He smiled, but beneath the grin she glimpsed weariness.

"Tough meeting?" she asked, remembering he said that morning he had one at the school in the afternoon.

"A long one, but I think we worked everything out for Jason to begin school this week."

"Good." She started forward.

Shane fell into step beside her. "How was your day?"

"Long."

"And starting with a wreck probably wasn't the best way to begin it."

She chuckled. "You think?" She'd called about the bus schedule and found one stopped not too far from the school so she would have a means of transportation to and from work until her car was fixed.

Whitney exited the building into the hot August day. Not a breeze stirred. Perspiration ran in rivulets down her face. She wiped her hand across her forehead then cheeks.

"Can I give you a ride anywhere?"

She glanced from the bus stop to Shane's SUV.

With the suffocating one-hundred-degree weather, she decided to be practical. "Sure. Thanks. I'm going to Noah's."

She slid into the passenger seat. At odd times during the day she'd thought about Dr. Shane McCoy, patiently working to help his son understand or reassuring her he'd take care of everything. But mostly she had remembered the concern in his green eyes that sparked something she'd been sure she had buried years ago. Living on the streets as a teenager had quickly persuaded her not to trust anyone and to do everything herself. She'd compromised some while living at her brother's estate, but she was going to change that when she moved out. Compromising meant giving up part of herself, and she didn't intend to do that ever again.

"Was everything all right when you arrived late?" Shane asked as he pulled out of the parking space.

"Yeah. Did you ever get Jason into the building?" She'd never been comfortable with chitchat, but with Noah's large family she'd had to learn quickly, especially with Lindsay, the only girl, following her around.

Disappointment glinted in his eyes. He shook his head. "On the bright side, Jason seemed to like the playground. He loved the yellow-seated swing and tunnels to crawl through. I had a hard time getting him to leave."

"So he hasn't seen his classroom?"

"No, maybe tomorrow."

"What will you do if he won't go in?"

"I'll take it one step at a time. With Jason that's all I can do. He's my son."

The love that filled his words made her study his profile presented to her as he drove toward her brother's estate. Strong. Steady. Full of compassion. Those traits had come to mind when she'd thought about Dr. Shane McCoy. Nothing like her own father. She pushed thoughts of that man from her mind; she tried not to go there.

"But still it must be hard." She found herself wanting to know what made someone like Shane tick. The men she had known had been people users, thinking only of themselves. Except Noah and his two foster brothers, Peter and Jacob. They were different. But weren't they the exception, not the rule? Certainly from her experience they were.

Shane didn't say anything for a good minute while he parked the SUV at the side of Noah's house. Then he turned to her with a smile deep in his eyes, the color of a lush patch of grass on a spring day. "The challenges of life are what make it interesting. I was blessed the day the Lord gave me Jason. He has made me a better person, and yes, it can be hard at times, but it makes me appreciate each step forward."

"So you're one of those people. When life gives you lemons, you make lemonade."

He chuckled. "I guess I am. I like lemonade."

Well, she didn't. She wanted something better than constantly struggling. Although she'd fought the decision to come to Cimarron City last November, to be involved in Noah's family, it had been a good one for her at the time. She needed to start fresh and do something with her life. And her brother's children had caused a dream from childhood to resurface. She wanted to be a teacher and would be one day.

"How long will it take for your car to be fixed?" Shane asked.

"I should have it by the end of the week."

"How are you going to get to—"

She held up her hand to stop his question. "I've got it figured out. The bus runs between here and the school. It's a pretty direct route."

He frowned. "How direct?"

"I only have to walk a few blocks. No big deal."

"In this heat? It's eighty at seven in the morning and over one hundred in the afternoon. I can give—"

"Don't. I'm a tough cookie. I can't let a wreck

stop me." She sent him a grin that he immediately responded to.

"Okay. Okay, I give up. I won't say another word. I think I've met my match in you."

Her grin grew as she opened the door, the searing heat invading the car's cool interior. "I'll take that as a compliment. Thanks again for the ride."

Under the shade of a large oak near the guest-house, she watched him turn around and head toward the gate that automatically opened at his approach. She could see why the children he counseled responded to him. His caring nature shone through even when dealing with a situation like that morning.

And he's easy on the eyes. His supple move-ments reminded her of a person who worked out. His large frame—muscular without an ounce of fat—confirmed that impression. The only thing unruly about him was his medium-length, coal-black hair that curled at his nape.

Perfect. That sent her alarms off. What was wrong with him? What was he hiding? Because her experience told her there was always some-thing that would rear its ugly head and throw her for a loop.

Even in the shade, the heat drove Whitney toward the guesthouse as soon as Shane's SUV disappeared from view. With coursework to get through and volunteering at Stone's Refuge this evening, she hoped she could sneak inside before one of the children, Noah or his wife, Cara, saw her and wanted her to recount her first day on the job.

Halfway across the yard, she heard a deep baritone voice call her name. She kept going. She knew what her brother wanted to talk about, and she wasn't ready to have that argument.

Escaping into the coolness of the guesthouse where she presently lived, she tossed her purse on the couch along with the section of the newspaper she'd taken to work. She hadn't gotten a chance to call Zoey Crandell; she needed to now before someone rented the place. After snatching the paper off the couch, she noted the number and picked up the receiver. As she punched in a five, a knock sounded at her door. She continued entering the phone number, hoping her brother would go away.

"You can't hide from this discussion, Whitney."

Noah's deep, commanding voice penetrated her haven. She sighed, hung up and crossed the room to open the door. "How about postponing it until I can string several words together to counter your arguments?"

"And give you the advantage?" He came inside. "Why are you looking for an apartment?"

She put her hands on her hips. "I'd say it's about

time. I should have gotten one seven or eight months ago." The previous November she'd come here from Dallas after quitting a dead-end job and leaving a man she'd been dating casually who had made the mistake of striking her. She wouldn't fall into that again. Ever. Instead, she'd taken her brother up on his invitation to spend the holidays with him and his family. And by the time the New Year had rolled around, she'd fallen in love with Noah's children, and for the first time in twenty years she had really been part of a family.

"But I just found you. Why are you leaving? The kids love having you here and so does Cara. Don't you want to be here to see your new nephew grow up? Taylor's only three months old."

"I'm not leaving Cimarron City. I'll be around, but on my terms." When she'd first come, she had intended to leave and move on to someplace where she could get lost in a crowd. She hadn't reckoned with the lure of Noah and his family.

"Why? You have family now. People who care about you."

"You, of all people, know I'm used to being on my own." She relaxed her arms, letting the tension slip from her shoulders. It took too much energy to have this conversation. "This isn't up for discussion anymore. I've let you persuade me to stick around just a little longer many times. And now I've been living in your guesthouse nine months."

"Why waste your hard-earned money on rent?"

Whitney blew out a frustrated breath. "I'll still be around and if you need a babysitter, I hope you'll ask me first. Coming back to Cimarron City, getting to know you and your family has changed so much for me, but I'm losing myself here. I've got to figure out who I am."

Noah frowned. "I guess I can't fault you for that. I know what it's like to grapple with yourself. For years I thought I wanted a certain lifestyle, but Cara convinced me that wasn't the case."

"Thank goodness she did. You're great as a father. Nothing like the one we had. Any child would be lucky to have you as a dad." She couldn't keep the wistful tone from her voice and wasn't surprised by it. She had never had loving parents— not even with the adoption situation she'd ended up in. At sixteen, Noah had had the Hendersons to show him the way; by the time she was sixteen she'd been living on the streets for six months.

"I'd better be. I have five children to take care of." Noah started for the door. "I'll let you rest. Isn't tonight one of the evenings you go to Stone's Refuge?"

"Yeah, I'll hitch a ride with Adam. He owes

me." Sometimes Noah's oldest adopted child rode with her.

"Hitch a ride? What about your car?"

"I was in a wreck this morning. It had to be towed to a garage to be fixed."

Noah's mouth fell open. "Why didn't you call? Say anything before now?"

"Why should I? I took care of everything."

"But—but we're family. We care. Were you hurt?"

"I'm fine. A little sore, but nothing I can't handle. Actually you know the owner of the vehicle I hit. Well, I didn't exactly hit him while he was in it. His car was parked in front of his house."

"Who?"

"Shane McCoy."

Noah's brow furrowed. "How did you hit his parked car?"

"To avoid hitting his son who had run into the street."

"Ah, Jason. Shane has his hands full." Noah put his hand on the doorknob. "You can use one of our cars if you need to."

"I have everything worked out."

Noah grumbled about her determination and opened the door. "We're eating at six. Coming up to the main house for dinner?"

"No, I'm gonna grab a sandwich before heading

over to the refuge with Adam. I have homework after that."

"It's okay to accept help, Whitney. We all need it from time to time."

When her brother left, Whitney plopped down in the chair at the kitchen table to call Zoey Crandell. She didn't want to live in an apartment complex with tons of people, so she hoped this place would work out for her.

Her cat came out of the bedroom and leaped into her lap, purring. "Calico, what am I gonna do about my brother?" Her pet settled down while she stroked the animal's back. "I already owe him too much. Being here has made me realize my life has to change. Now I have to figure out exactly what I want without him doing everything for me."

Again resolved to make that call about the garage apartment, she was halfway through entering the number when another knock interrupted her. By the sound of it she was sure it was Lindsay.

"Come in," Whitney called out, again hanging up the phone.

The little girl who Cara and Noah adopted along with her two older brothers swung the door open wide. Calico stirred, peered at the seven-year-old and hopped down to greet her before finding a spot in the windowsill to peer out.

Dressed in her bathing suit, Lindsay hugged a towel to her chest. "Will ya watch me swim?"

Whitney glanced at her clock on the stove. "I can for a while."

Lindsay beamed. "I can always count on you."

"First, I have a call to make."

"Can't it wait?"

"No." Whitney picked up the phone and finally placed her call to Zoey Crandell, setting up a time to see the apartment.

"Are you leaving here?" Lindsay screwed her face into a pout.

Whitney hung up the receiver. "Yes, but I won't be too far away. You can't get rid of me that easily."

"You'll come and watch me swim?"

"Of course." When Whitney neared the child, Lindsay grabbed her hand and tugged her outside. "Hold it. What's the rush? We do have some time."

"I've gotta practice my swimming. I want to be the best."

At the pool behind the main house, Whitney sat on the edge, adjusting her split skirt so she could stick her legs into the water without it getting wet. She relished the feel of the coolness on her tired, aching feet.

After the little girl swam a few laps, trying out various strokes, she came to the side where Whitney perched and clung to the tile lip. "Now that I'm a Maxwell, I've been thinking I should call you Aunt Whitney. May I?"

The question stunned Whitney. She had never expected to have nieces and nephews—until she'd come to Cimarron City. She'd always thought of herself going through life alone. Emotions jammed her throat. She never cried, not since she'd been separated from Noah as a child, and yet the tears swelled up from the depths of her being.

"Whitney?"

The child's expression, full of worry, forced Whitney to say something and yet she wasn't sure her voice would work. She peered away, staring at the gazebo near the pond. A tear slipped down her face. She swiped it away.

Clearing her throat, she finally said, "I'd love for you to."

Lindsay pulled herself out of the pool and flung herself into Whitney's arms. "You're the bestest aunt. I love you."

The scent of chlorine peppered the air. That must be why another tear coursed down her cheek. She kissed the top of Lindsay's wet hair, swallowing hard. "I love you, too, Lindsay." What would it be like to have her own child?

That question nibbled at her mind, but she determinedly shoved it away. Instead, she cherished this moment because this would be the closest she would come to having a family and children. She would have to content herself with her niece and nephews because she would never have a child of her own who would depend on her.

At work two days later, Whitney hung up the phone after talking with a man at the garage where her car was being fixed. Turning away from the counter at the main entrance into the building, she spied Shane trying to coax Jason inside. School started the next day, and it didn't look as if things were going well with Jason adjusting to a new situation. Yesterday she didn't think the child had come into the building, either.

Before she realized it, her legs carried her toward the double doors and outside. "Hi, Shane. Jason."

Her words disrupted the boy's whine. When he stopped yanking on his father's arm to get him to leave, he quit shaking his head and stared at her. Then suddenly he launched himself at her.

She stood her ground.

"Pretty yellow hair."

Whitney bent toward Jason, the movement of dropping her head slightly intensified the ache in her neck caused by the accident a few days ago. She would curl up with the heating pad again that evening when she got home from seeing the apartment. She intended to grab the garage apartment at Zoey Crandell's and move in as soon as possible, hopefully this weekend.

"What's going on, Jason? Have you checked out your new classroom yet?"

The child focused on her ponytail, which had fallen forward.

"Not yet. I was hoping today," Shane said while his son remained silent but continued to touch her hair. "Is that okay?" He gestured toward what Jason was doing.

"Fine." After a minute, she straightened, holding her hand out to the child. She'd made a point the day before to see who would be Jason's teacher. "I can show you to your classroom. I know they have a yellow ball in there." Jason's face started to screw up into a scowl until she mentioned the toy.

"Yellow ball!" He dragged her toward the door into the building.

"I guess we're going inside," she said over her shoulder as Shane followed them into the lobby.

She guided the pair down the first long hallway on the right and stopped at the second room. Jason came to a halt when he saw his teacher a few feet from him, tacking up a poster by the door. Suddenly he hid his face against Shane.

"Mrs. Bradley, this is Jason and his father, Shane McCoy. Jason was interested in seeing your yellow ball."

The older teacher approached them with a neutral expression. She shook Shane's hand. "It's nice to see you again. I see you were able to get Jason inside."

"Not me. Whitney did."

That she had awed Whitney. When she had decided to go for her degree in elementary education, she'd never dreamed of dealing with children who had special needs like Jason. Only in the past few months with her interaction with Noah's four adopted children, coupled with her volunteer work at Stone's Refuge, had she realized she wanted to work with kids. But a child with special needs? For years she'd been drifting from one job to the next—just trying to make a living and staying off the streets.

"Yellow ball?" Jason asked, his words muffled against his father.

"Oh, that. Jason, it's over in the corner." Mrs. Bradley pointed to the left.

The child peeked around his father, saw it and tore across the room to stroke it.

The teacher faced Shane. "I still have my reservations about this working. We just aren't equipped for a child like Jason here at this school. He should be in a self-contained special education class like at Eisenhower Elementary School."

"I insist on trying this. We won't know until we

do. I signed the paperwork for him to be in special education, but I want him involved with all kinds of children. We're working on socialization at home and with his therapist. I'll keep you informed of things that develop at home, and I want you to keep me informed about what's going on here." A firm resolve underscored each of Shane's words.

Although Whitney faced Jason playing with the ball, her attention focused on the exchange between Shane and the teacher. Just the few times she'd been around the boy, Whitney couldn't imagine what it was like to deal with a child with Jason's obvious limitations. And yet, Shane did it with love and patience. How was Jason going to fit into a normal kindergarten class, especially with a teacher who was less than enthusiastic?

"I have a meeting to attend. You and your son may stay for a while and get familiar with the classroom if you wish." Mrs. Bradley slipped off a smock she wore to protect her clothes while cleaning.

After the teacher left, Shane turned to Whitney. "Thanks for helping earlier. I'd about run out of ideas on how to get Jason into the building. You saved the day."

Her first instinct was to scoff at his compliment. In the past people only gave them to get something from her. Then she remembered Lindsay telling her she was the best aunt a few days ago. Noah and his family were chipping away at all her defenses she'd learned to use over the years.

"You're welcome," she managed to say after a long pause. She took a step back, not sure what to do with her changing attitude. "I'd better get back to the office. I was unpacking some new supplies."

"I was going to call you," Shane said as she turned to leave.

She stopped and glanced back at him.

"Remember I need to pay the deductible. When will your car be ready to pick up?"

"Friday afternoon."

"I can pick you up at school, take you to the garage and pay my part."

"You don't have to go to all that trouble. Just write a check to Premier Body Shop and I'll give it to them."

Shane's gaze riveted to hers. "If that's the way you want it." He removed his checkbook and quickly wrote a check for her.

Beneath her brave front, he glimpsed vulnerability in Whitney that he doubted she knew she projected. But he'd seen it in a lot of the children he'd worked with over the years. What had put it there for Whitney?

He looked toward his son, rolling the ball around the floor in the corner. He had enough problems raising a child with autism. Since his wife had died five years ago, his hands had been full just making it through each day as a single dad. He certainly didn't need to become involved with anyone.

But there was something in her brown eyes that haunted him, even invading his dreams at night.

Saturday morning, Whitney dragged herself to the kitchen to make coffee and grab something to eat before she tackled packing the boxes to move. While the coffee brewed, she hurriedly dressed in navy blue shorts and a red T-shirt and was back in time to pour a huge mug of the hot liquid, its aroma spicing the air.

As she sat at the table and ate her bowl of cereal, she looked around at the mess she'd created the night before in preparation for her move this weekend. Her gaze lit upon a yellow pillow that graced the sofa, and she immediately thought about Jason. He hadn't attended school either Thursday or Friday. She'd almost called Shane on Friday to see if his son was all right. She'd even dialed halfway through the phone number before she'd slammed down the receiver, determined not to intrude.

Finally yesterday afternoon she'd asked Mrs. Bradley if she knew why Jason wasn't at school.

She'd said that he had come for about fifteen minutes the day before with his father and thirty that morning to acquaint himself more with the classroom. But he left when Dr. McCoy did. Disappointment had spread over Whitney as she'd gone back to the classroom she'd been assigned to assist in.

She wanted Jason's school experience to work. That was the only reason she'd been disappointed the day before. Taking a long sip of her coffee, she shut down her thoughts about Shane and his son. Getting involved with them wasn't a smart move. She already had too much on her plate—starting with packing.

A few minutes later as she emptied another drawer of her possessions, someone knocked at her door. She was trying to decide which member of the family was going to tell her all the reasons she shouldn't move.

When she swung the door open, she was surprised that every member of Noah's family, except the baby, stood outside the guesthouse. "I don't want anyone of you to say another word about my move. If that's why you came en masse, turn around and leave. I've got too much to do to listen."

Noah grinned. "We're here to help you. I've got Peter and Jacob coming to help with moving the pieces of furniture. They're bringing a van.

And Jacob's wife is watching the baby so we're all free to help all day."

Free all day! The gesture touched Whitney but at the same time overwhelmed her—as usual. "But the furniture is yours. Zoey has a few pieces in the apartment, and I was going to buy some when I save up enough money."

"Nope," Cara said as she came forward, "we decided to redecorate the guesthouse. This won't fit with the new scheme." She waved her hand at the surroundings.

"No, this is yours."

Lindsay gasped at Whitney's fierce tone. Rusty's eyes widened as Whitney faced her brother.

"Guys, let's start in the bedroom with packing," Cara said, gathering the four children and pushing them toward the back of the guesthouse.

When the room was cleared of everyone but Noah and Whitney, he released a long breath and frowned. "Haven't you figured out what's mine is yours? You are my family. I don't need this furniture. You do. Why spend money on something I can give you?"

She narrowed her eyes on her brother. "Because I don't want your handouts. I'm twenty-eight years old. I'm going to do this on my own."

"Cara taught me that you don't have to go through life alone, that it's okay to need others."

"That's you, not me."

He glared at her for a long moment. "Can we compromise on this? You use the furniture until you can replace it with your own, then you can give the pieces to charity. Okay?"

There was that word *compromise* again. In his eyes she saw the need for her to say yes. Noah did too much for her, but she'd found out from Cara not long after she'd come to town that it was important to her brother to help his little sister. That was part of the reason she'd stayed longer than she had intended. Noah's guilt over not being able to find her for years still ate at him. He'd felt it was his fault her childhood had been rough, that he hadn't been able to protect her.

"Fine, but just until I can buy my own."

The huge smile that spread over her brother's features told her she had made the right decision. Okay, as much as she didn't want to compromise anymore in her life, she had to be realistic. There would be a few occasions when she would have to. But she would control when and what.

That evening in her new apartment, surrounded by chaos, she sat among the unopened boxes and knew she would have a lot to do tomorrow. She'd refused Noah's offer to bring her something to eat because she'd craved some quiet time after being among the whole family plus a few friends. Although they'd wanted to help her put some of her items away, she needed to do that personally.

Exhausted as she was, maybe she should have accepted the assistance. But she had a hard time letting others do things for her. She always expected them to have their hand out for something in return. Although Noah's family hadn't done that, old habits were hard to break.

When someone rapped on her front door, she jumped, her gaze swinging toward it. With a quick peek at her watch noting the still early time, she strode toward the entrance. Must be Zoey. But when she checked the peephole, the fading sunlight, as it headed toward the western horizon, illuminated Shane McCoy.

Chapter Three

$\sim$

Whitney automatically glanced down at her wrinkled attire, dirty from moving all day, and frowned. When she found herself finger-combing her hair, her anger rose. Why did she care how she looked? She looked like a person who had been working hard.

She wrenched the door open, ready to tell Shane she was too tired for company. The instant she saw his smiling face, then Jason next to him, both holding containers of what appeared to have food in them, the words fled her mind. Even covered, the aroma wafting from the dishes made her stomach rumble.

"We saw Noah leaving while Jason and I were going for our bike ride. He said you moved in today and grumbled something about you didn't have much food yet, so how did you think you were going to eat tonight? So here we are with your dinner. Aunt Louise always makes too much for just us to eat." Shane held up his casserole dish. "It's pot roast with vegetables. And Jason has a salad. If you aren't hungry right now, it can hold until tomorrow."

At that moment her stomach growled. "I guess that's your answer. I'm hungry. Come in, you two."

"I don't want to impose. I just wanted to bring by a welcome-to-the-neighborhood gift."

Jason finally peered up at her, his gaze lighting up when it encountered her hair, which she'd taken down from her ponytail a while ago. "Pretty." Moving into the apartment, he touched the strands that had fallen forward over her shoulder.

"Well, I guess we'll come in." Shane crossed the threshold, taking the container from his son. "Where do you want these?"

"Kitchen." She gestured toward the area off the living room while making her way toward one of the few places she could sit in the apartment.

When she settled on the sofa, Jason took the seat by her and occasionally grazed his fingers across her hair. When the boy's gaze fell upon Calico perched on a box, he leaped to his feet, hurrying toward the cat. Her pet watched the child's quick approach but remained put. Jason picked up Calico, burying his face in her fur.

"Is that okay?"

"Sure, Calico loves kids. She had to learn fast when she was at the refuge and with Noah's children."

Empty-handed now, Shane approached her. "We won't stay. It wasn't that long ago I moved into our house and know how tired you have to be."

"You two have had dinner?"

"Yeah, before we headed out on our bike adventure."

Jason caught sight of a box with some yellow lettering on it. Hopping up with the cat cradled in his arms, he made a beeline for the container and traced the colored words on the cardboard.

"I noticed Jason wasn't in class on Friday when I stopped by."

"We're taking it a little bit at a time. I'm hoping I'll be able to leave him sometime next week."

"You sound like you expected it to go faster."

"I can always hope. He's been doing well with his therapist, and there are even times he can handle a little change in plans." Shane lounged back against some boxes stacked along the wall with his arms crossed over his chest. "But I know this isn't a little change. He needs a reason to want to stay."

"I could meet you on Monday and escort you two to the classroom, maybe distract him while you leave. What else does Jason like besides yellow and cats?"

"Actually any kind of animal."

"That's wonderful. Mrs. Bradley told me she was getting a rabbit over the weekend for the class. Maybe I could get him involved with the rabbit."

"That might be enough."

"Has he ever gone out to Stone's Refuge to the barn with the animals?"

Shane shook his head.

"You ought to take him. Peter and Laura have a wonderful collection of all kinds of animals, mostly abandoned and in need of love." Was that the reason she was drawn to Stone's Refuge and the barn? There had been so many times in her life she'd felt that way. Stone's Refuge was a place where children for whom the state couldn't find foster parents were placed.

"I'll have to ask Peter about visiting with Jason when I'm out there next time."

"Do you go often?" She'd never seen him there even though she'd known he worked with some of the kids.

"Occasionally, especially when I want to see a child I'm counseling in his normal environment." Shane pushed to an erect stance. "We'd better let you eat. It's getting close to Jason's bedtime and his ritual takes a while to get him ready to go to sleep."

Whitney stood. "It sounds like routines are important with Jason."

"Yes, but then with most children they are, just more so with him." Shane turned toward his son. "Jason." He didn't continue until he had his child's attention. "We need to go home, buddy." Shane strode to the front door and opened it, then waited for Jason to put down the cat.

Reluctantly, his son let go of Calico and hurried out of the apartment and down the stairs.

"Good night, Whitney, and welcome to the neighborhood."

"Thanks for the dinner."

Shane followed Jason who paused next to Whitney's car and ran his hand along its length.

Swinging around and backpedaling, Shane looked up at her. "Was it fixed okay?"

"Yes. Actually I think it runs even better," she said, leaning against the wooden railing on her small porch.

"That's wonderful. At least something good came out of what happened on Monday." Shane faced forward and took his son's hand before heading across the street toward his house.

Whitney watched them until they disappeared from her view, the dim light of dusk settling over the neighborhood. The August heat of an Oklahoma day still lingered in the air. A cardinal chirped in a nearby maple, its bright red coloring vivid among the green foliage. The scent of the honeysuckle bush beneath her porch along the side of the garage sweetened the warm breeze that blew.

The move today had made her aware of just how much her life was changing—like Jason's. Maybe they could help each other through the change.

Returning from the grocery store after coming home from church, Shane drove past Whitney's apartment, his gaze straying to it. Was she busy unpacking? He remembered all the unopened boxes stacked in her living area the night before. Did she need help? Was her family going to help today?

He had to agree with his son about her hair. The color was a rich, deep gold. It fell in thick waves about her shoulders, inviting a person to caress it as if it were a waterfall of sunshine.

And why in the world was he even thinking about her? She had a Do Not Disturb sign hanging around her neck. She didn't trust others. He knew that in his gut because he had recognized the defensive signs, a certain wary look in the eye, an "I want to do everything myself" attitude, because trusting meant putting yourself out there to be hurt.

He also knew a little about not trusting. When Becka, his pregnant wife, had been killed in a house fire, he'd gone through a period where he'd backed away from family and friends. Then Aunt Louise had appeared at his doorstep and shown him the importance of trusting in the Lord. Once he had turned to Him, the rest fell into place. Yes, there were times he was disappointed in others or hurt by them, but the alternative was worse— cutting yourself off from people, especially the ones who really cared about you. But having been deeply in love with his wife, he never wanted to feel that kind of loss ever again.

He was perfectly content to focus on Jason. He'd grown to appreciate his son and his unique perspective on life. Jason was his life now.

So why couldn't he stop thinking about Whitney?

Pushing the question from his mind, he parked in his driveway and climbed from his vehicle. He grabbed the sack with bread and strawberry jam he'd gotten at the store for his aunt so she could fix Jason's lunch and headed toward the front door. Inside silence greeted him. Too quiet. Usually the radio in the kitchen was going or the television in the den. Or Jason was jabbering to his aunt or one of his toys.

Had Aunt Louise taken Jason out? Shane moved toward the kitchen, his aunt's domain and where she spent a lot of time. Just inside the door Shane glimpsed his son in the den, sitting cross-legged on the hardwood floor, rocking back and forth with a broad grin on his face. Shane's gaze swept the kitchen. No Aunt Louise.

Moving toward the den, he scanned that room. His gaze came to an abrupt halt a foot from his son. Hidden from his earlier perusal Aunt Louise lay on the area carpet.

Shane raced to her and felt her pulse. He breathed a sigh when he got one. Digging in his pocket for his cell, he punched in 9-1-1 while he looked over at his son to make sure he was all right. Jason still smiled, as though nothing was wrong. In his mind it wasn't.

After giving the operator the necessary information and asking that the siren not be used within a few blocks of the street, he turned to his son again. Sirens, like thunder, would upset Jason.

"Why don't you go watch Animal Planet in my bedroom?" Shane didn't want him to witness the EMTs taking Aunt Louise away.

"Can Auntie watch?"

Knowing Jason, when someone's eyes were closed, he would think she was sleeping, not hurt. "Maybe later."

As his son left the den, Aunt Louise's eyes fluttered open. She stared at Shane, her forehead wrinkling. "What am…" She tried to rise to a sitting position but instead wilted back against the carpet. "Why—am I—on the floor?" she murmured, bringing her hand to her head and covering her eyes for a few seconds.

"That's a good question. You don't remember?"

Her hand slid away from her face. "I— No."

A few minutes later when the doorbell rang, Shane sighed. "That's the paramedics. I called 9-1-1. Be right back." He hurried to the front door and let the two EMTs inside. "She's in the den. She's awake now but groggy."

"What happened?" the tall one asked.

"I don't know and neither does she."

"Is she diabetic? Have a heart condition?"

"No, not that I know of. The only thing she's had problems with is arthritis in her knees."

Shane hung back while the EMTs worked on Aunt Louise and put her on the stretcher. Before they wheeled her out the door, Shane took his aunt's hand. "I'll be right behind the ambulance. They'll take good care of you."

"I'll be fine. I'm in the Lord's hands."

The second the ambulance pulled away, Shane went to get Jason. He'd rather not take him to the hospital, but he didn't want to take the time to find a babysitter. What if his aunt had had a heart attack and had another one before he could get there? He didn't want her to be alone. He owed her so much.

When Shane went upstairs and into his bedroom to round up Jason, it was empty. He checked the master bathroom, then went to Jason's room across the hall. Again his son was nowhere in sight. Trying to remain calm, he hurried through the rest of the house, calling his son's name over and over.

Fifteen minutes later, frantic, he headed out the kitchen door to see if Jason was in the backyard. The phone rang, the sound jerking Shane back around and into the house. He snatched it up while glancing out the bay window in the breakfast nook.

"Shane, this is Whitney. Jason showed up at my apartment. He was downstairs touching my car. I figured you didn't know he came over."

He collapsed into the chair nearby, dropping his head in relief. "No, I didn't. I'll be right over."

When Whitney opened the door to reveal Shane on her stoop, her heart twisted at the sight of the man, pale, his hair tousled, his expression drawn and worn.

"I called you as soon as I saw him." Whitney stepped to the side to allow him to enter.

"I really appreciate that. This hasn't been a good day." Shane's gaze slipped from her to find his son on the couch, writing on a yellow pad while Calico pressed up against his thigh.

"He's drawing a picture of my cat for me."

Whitney closed the door and moved toward her kitchen area, the sound of Jason's pencil strokes and Calico purring echoing through the apartment. "I know it's almost one, but do you want some coffee?"

"No, I can't stay. Aunt Louise was just taken to the hospital in an ambulance."

The love and concern for his aunt filled Shane's eyes and tugged at her. That was what she and her brother were beginning to develop. "What happened?"

"I came home from going to the store and found her on the floor in the den, passed out. I don't know what happened, and when she came to, she didn't, either." Shane stepped closer and lowered his voice. "I sent Jason into another room so he wouldn't see the paramedics take my aunt away. He left the house instead. I didn't even hear the front door opening. When I couldn't find him…" What little color he had leached completely from his face.

The urge to comfort strong, Whitney placed her hand on his arm. "I'm so sorry. I can only imagine the horror of finding your child gone." And he still had his aunt to see about. "Let me help you. I can watch Jason while you go to the hospital if you want."

"I can't ask you to do that. Look at all you have to do." He gestured at the stacked boxes.

"First, you didn't ask me. I'm volunteering, and I don't volunteer unless I want to. Second, I have to go to Stone's Refuge today, and I think Jason would enjoy it. I want to show him the animals in the barn."

"You're going to the farm when you have all this to unpack?"

"I do every Sunday afternoon, and this will be here when I get back. It isn't going anywhere." She grinned, remembering how neat and tidy his home was and wondering if it was Shane more than Aunt Louise.

"I can't imagine living out of boxes for more than a day. I don't do well with chaos."

"And I have acquired more chaos than I thought possible this past year." Because her brother had showered her with gifts until she'd had to cry uncle. "Chaos, that is, if I emptied every one of these," her arm swept toward the stacks in the living area, "and didn't put anything away. However, a little chaos is okay sometimes."

He arched an eyebrow. "If you say so."

"Has Jason eaten?"

"No, in fact, that's why I made an emergency run to the store. He had gotten into the jam and bread sometime since yesterday so there wasn't any for a sandwich for him."

"What does Jason like to eat?"

"Two things. Peanut butter and strawberry jam or a hamburger from Lucky's Drive Thru."

"Oh, he has good taste. Nothing beats Lucky's hamburger. Don't tell Noah I said that."

"I'm trying to expand my son's tastes to other foods, but I've not had much success yet."

"That's all he eats?" Whitney again looked over at the boy who was still happily doodling on the yellow pad.

"For lunch. He'll only eat certain dishes for each meal."

"Interesting. I don't know much about autism."

"Routine and order is very important to him."

And to Shane? Her life had never had much routine or order to it. Since coming to Cimarron City, however, she'd acquired some of both.

"I'd better be going. I told Aunt Louise I would be there for her."

"Go. If I run into a problem, I'll let you know."

"If anything happens, I can be there in twenty minutes."

"It shouldn't. We'll go to Lucky's then Stone's Refuge. We'll be there most of the afternoon." She covered the few steps to her door while Shane strode to his son and knelt in front of him.

Clasping both upper arms, Shane waited until he had Jason's attention. "I need to leave for a while. Whitney is going to watch you. She's taking you to Lucky's for a hamburger then to see some animals at a farm. Okay?"

His son peered at her. "Like yellow hair." Then he dropped his head and began drawing again.

Shane came toward her. "I think everything will be all right. Call, if it's not. Aunt Louise will understand if I have to leave."

"Will do." Whitney stepped out onto the stoop with him. "Don't worry about him. If he loves animals, he'll enjoy the farm."

"Thanks." He glanced toward the entrance. "Are you sure about this?"

"My brother keeps telling me I need to learn to accept help. Guess what? You should, too."

He chuckled. "Yeah, my aunt tells me that. I've had to learn with Jason."

She turned him around and gently pushed him toward the stairs. "Go. Make sure Louise is all right."

Down below Shane peered up at her. "What if this takes longer—"

"Dr. McCoy, goodbye. I'm going inside." She determinedly pivoted away from him and headed back inside, but before closing the door, she glimpsed him jogging away. What happened to Shane's wife? How had she died? There was a lot about him that was appealing and attractive. Were Jason and his problems the reason Shane hadn't remarried? Or something else? It was clear he hadn't moved on after five years because he still wore his wedding ring. Did he use it like a suit of armor to protect himself?

She wouldn't ask those questions aloud. It wasn't her business. But that didn't stop her from wondering about them.

The second they entered the barn at Stone's Refuge, Jason saw a large mutt near the tool room, eating his food from a metal bowl. The boy raced toward the dog before Whitney could grab him and hold him back. Plopping down on all fours by the animal, Jason stared at it. The mutt fixed his gaze on the child, only a few inches separated their noses.

Whitney started forward to get Shane's son before the dog bit him. A hand stopped her. She glanced back at Peter Stone, the man who had founded Stone's Refuge for children in the foster-care system. He and Noah had bonded while they lived together in a foster home as teens.

"Wait, see what the dog does. He's been gentle and good so far with the kids here."

"I didn't see him last week. How long has he been here?"

"About five days, but you should have seen Jacob's son hanging off him yesterday. Took it like he'd been doing it all his life."

The mutt and Jason assessed each other for a good three minutes before the dog buried his head in his bowl and ate his food. Still down on all fours, the boy just watched and waited. When the mutt finished with his meal, he swung toward Jason and licked his face. The child laughed.

That sound, loud and robust, wormed its way into Whitney's heart.

"Are you going riding with the kids today?"

Since the spring when Peter had taught her to ride a horse, she'd been going with a group of children from the refuge each Sunday afternoon and whenever she could work some time into her schedule. "I don't know with Shane's son here."

"I can watch him. Shane goes to my church, and I've been around Jason for the past several years. But maybe he'll want to go riding, too."

"Does he know how?"

"Not that I know of. He's never been here, and Shane's hasn't said anything to me about it."

"Then is that a good idea?"

Peter nodded toward the child. "It's obvious he loves animals."

Jason patted the mutt, rubbing his face against the dog's.

"You know how good animals are therapeutically. Why do you think I keep so many? The kids here respond to them, often before they do with an adult at the refuge."

"Yeah." She'd known personally how they were for her. There was a connection between her and certain animals she couldn't explain. Being with them was calming. When she rode, she didn't think about her problems. She just enjoyed the experience. And Calico was whom she told all her troubles to.

"You don't have to go far from the barn. The other children won't mind. You're taking the younger ones today." Peter started toward a stall. "We have some time before the other kids arrive. Let's see what Jason does on a horse."

A minute later Peter brought a small chestnut horse out into the main part of the barn and put a saddle on it. The movement caught Jason's attention. Still on all fours, the boy's eyes followed everything that Peter did.

Whitney covered the distance between her and Jason. "Would you like to ride with me in the paddock?"

His large brown gaze fastened onto her. He took her hand and led her toward the horse.

"I guess that's a yes," she said with a laugh.

Whitney quickly retrieved the gray mare she always rode from a stall and prepped her. She'd fallen in love with Princess Leia the first time she'd come to the barn last December. The mare's previous owner had abused the horse, but with a lot of love, Whitney had won the animal over. After securing the leather straps around her middle, she dug into her pocket and removed the carrot she'd brought to give to Princess Leia. They were kindred spirits.

Whitney scratched her behind her ear, something she'd discovered the mare enjoyed. "Are you ready? I've missed you this week. I didn't get to come see you Wednesday evening. I was helping out at a cottage. Hannah was short staffed."

When she looked toward Peter to see if Jason had mounted and was ready, she discovered the child's gaze focused on her, taking in everything she did. She smiled at the boy who still hadn't gotten into the saddle.

"Okay, Jason. Let's get you up on Big Red." Peter moved to help the child mount.

Jason scrambled to Whitney's side and clung to her. "Let me see if I can get him up. He doesn't know you." There was a part of her that was amazed she said that as though she really knew Jason well.

She led the boy back to Big Red and patted the gelding's side. "Jason, you can pat him, too, just like Calico."

Tentatively the boy reached out and brushed his

fingertips over the chestnut's coat. Jason giggled and looked up at Whitney. Her hands about the child's small waist, she lifted him onto the horse.

Clutching the saddle horn, Jason squealed with delight, never taking his eyes off Whitney. She swung onto her mare.

As she rode next to Jason around the paddock, she held the reins to his horse. He wouldn't let go of the saddle horn, but he beamed with a huge grin and occasionally laughed. As before, the sound was sweet like the mockingbird in a nearby tree. A breeze kicked up, cooling the warmth of the summer sun.

When she came to a halt by the gate into the paddock, she shifted in the saddle toward Jason. "Do you want to go riding in that field?"

He glanced toward where she pointed. "Go, horsie."

Four children, ranging in ages from seven to eleven, accompanied her and Jason on their ride to the stream. Shane's son stuck right next to her. He never let go of the saddle horn, and when they arrived at the brook, he wouldn't dismount.

"Whitney, look what I found," Andy Morgan said, running up to her with a baby turtle in the palm of his hand. "He was all alone by the water. I think he's lost from his mother."

"Baby turtles don't stay with their mother."

He screwed his face into a worried look. "They don't? Then who looks out for them?"

"They do for themselves."

"Kinda like I did before my mom got better?"

"Yep." Although Andy now lived with his mother, for several years before, he'd been in a cottage at the refuge because of Lisa's drug problem. Lisa and she had immediately become friends because Whitney recognized a kindred soul in Lisa. And like Andy, she'd learned to look out for herself as a child. "I'm sure glad your mom was able to bring you to ride with us."

"Me, too. She went to the cottage to talk with Hannah. I'm supposed to walk back with the others when we're finished. Are you and Jason gonna come with us?"

Whitney peered up at Jason, who had leaned over and was stroking the chestnut horse. "We'll see." Checking the time, she announced to the three other children by the water, "We'd better head back to the barn. Supper will be soon."

After all the kids mounted their rides, Whitney took the reins of Jason's gelding and started back. As she neared the barn, she saw Shane pacing in front of the large entrance, his strides long and purposeful. He raked his hand continuously through his hair, a frown on his face.

Had something happened to his aunt?

Chapter Four

When Whitney reached the barn, she swung down from her mare and covered the short distance to Shane. "Is Louise all right?" she whispered so the children wouldn't overhear.

"She had a ministroke called a TIA. They're keeping her overnight for some tests and observation." One corner of his mouth eased into a grin. "She insisted I leave so she could get some rest."

"What did the doctor say about the TIA?"

"She'll be on medication and needs to take it easy, at least for a while."

"Go, horsie," Jason said as the other children headed their mounts into the barn.

Shane swung around toward his son who was bobbing up and down in the saddle while gripping the horn. Shane glanced back at Whitney. "How did you get him up on a horse?"

"Are you all right about him riding? He loved it."

"Is it safe?"

"He's a natural." Whitney strolled to Big Red and grabbed the dangling reins that had come loose from where she'd tied them on the saddle horn before the gelding stepped on them. "Jason, why don't you hold these while I lead you into the barn."

The boy stared at her but didn't move to take the reins.

"Or I can hold them," she mumbled, and escorted the child and horse through the large double doors. When she found some time, she would be doing some research on autism.

"Go, horsie, go."

Shane fell into step next to her. "The hard part may be getting Jason off the horse."

"I'd like to bring him out here to ride when I come on Sunday afternoons. I've heard of stables that have therapeutic riding for children with special needs."

Jason giggled as Big Red came to a stop near his stall.

"There's no way I could say no after hearing that laugh. He doesn't do that often enough."

"Go, horsie."

Whitney rounded the front of the gelding and stood at the side with her arms stretched up to help

Jason down as she had helped him earlier. "Time to get off Big Red. It's his dinnertime."

Jason clutched the horn even tighter.

His eyes tired-looking, Shane moved to Whitney and put his hand over his son's. "Jason, get down now." His voice was even, but firm.

When Jason remained still, staring straight ahead, Shane started to pull him from the saddle.

Whitney stopped him with a touch on his arm. "I think I have a way to get him down."

She hurried to the mutt Jason had interacted with earlier. The dog lay by the tack room, taking in everything around him. She knelt and rubbed him behind his ears. "I hope you'll help me with Jason." She stood and slapped her hand against her jeans-clad leg. "C'mon, boy."

The mixed breed followed her to Big Red. She sat on her haunches and petted the animal. "Jason, I think he misses you."

The child's eyes lit up when he saw the dog. He practically fell into his father's arms in his haste to get down. Shane steadied himself and clutched his son against him for a few seconds, then set the boy on the ground. Jason flew to the dog and got down on all fours to lock gazes with him.

Shane stepped to Whitney with a question in his eyes. "He bonded with him before he went riding?"

"Yep. I'm not sure you're gonna be able to leave

here without taking the dog with you. He needs a home." She slanted a look at Shane. "What do you think about that?"

"I kinda half expected it." He presented his right hand, palm up and said, "You've got Jason who loves animals." Then his left one appeared. "You've got a refuge for abandoned children and animals. I figured my son would fall in love with at least one animal. I'd been thinking of getting him a pet, and I'd rather take in a homeless one."

"Well, technically, he isn't homeless anymore. I haven't seen Peter turn one out even if he can't find a permanent place for the animal."

He laughed. "You think I should go to the pound instead?"

"No, believe me, Peter will be grateful to have one less animal. I've lost count how many he has. Of course, the number changes daily."

"How can people just discard pets when they get tired of them?"

"Or children?" She thought of the young people she'd encountered when she'd lived on the streets. Many, like her, had been driven from their homes for various reasons from abuse to drinking and drugs.

A frown carved deep lines into Shane's face. "I was trying not to think about that. Children are so precious. I don't know…" His expression went blank. Shane swallowed hard, then murmured, "Excuse me for a moment. I'll go see Peter about taking the dog."

Shane hurried toward the back exit. Whitney stared at the spot where he last was. He worked with children, some from the refuge. Was his reaction just a minute ago due to that or something else?

While Shane was gone and Jason was staring down the mutt, she removed the saddle from both the gelding and mare. She checked to make sure the other children were tending to their horses.

"Andy, will you walk Princess Leia for me?" she asked Lisa Morgan's son who had finished cooling down his mount.

"Sure. Are you coming with us to the cottage?"

"I told Hannah I'd stop by after we rode."

"Mom and I are staying for dinner at Hannah's. She makes the best spaghetti."

"That she does. She gave me the recipe, but mine doesn't turn out as well as hers."

When Andy left with her mare, Whitney, holding Big Red's reins, approached Shane's son. "Jason, we need to walk your horse to cool him off. It's hot out there."

Jason didn't say anything nor did he look at her. She decided not to push the issue with him since he was so focused on the mutt, but she always taught each child how to care for his mount before and after riding it. If she worked with Jason, she would teach him, too—when he was ready. She started for the back door.

Jason leaped to his feet and raced after her. She peered down at him. He'd heard. He even put his hands on the reins, too.

Emerging from the barn, Whitney caught sight of Shane talking with Peter in the paddock. The haggard look to Shane's features touched a core inside her. She didn't want to be attracted to him. Every relationship she'd had ended badly. She had either picked the wrong guy or she couldn't give the man what he wanted, a part of herself.

Finally when she had escaped Dallas for Cimarron City, she'd realized that she wasn't meant to fall in love. That was for people like her brother and Cara. By the time she'd arrived in town, she'd accepted that decision. New life. New plan and goals.

"Jason, we'll walk Big Red under that maple tree."

As she and the boy made their third circle around the trunk, Whitney let go of the reins to see if Jason would continue by himself. Big Red was the gentlest horse at the farm so she wasn't afraid anything would happen to the child.

Jason took one step then another. He peered toward her but kept going. Moving back a few paces, she observed his trek while the hairs on her nape tingled. With a glance over her shoulder, she saw Shane quickly covering the distance between them.

"Is that safe?" he asked, a dull flatness to his eyes.

"Jason will be fine. If you want to go home, I can bring him by later."

He shook his head. "I'll stay."

"It's hard to let go, isn't it?"

"Yeah. He reacts to things so differently than other children. Others don't understand. For that matter, I don't at times." He gave her a rueful smile. "But I'm learning. As a parent, I have no other choice."

Not true. Shane had a choice. She remembered her own father who had used his children as a punching bag until he up and left them to fend for themselves.

"After Jason's through, I was going to Hannah's with the other children. Why don't you two come with us? Get your mind off all that's happened today."

"I guess we can for a while." He faced her. "But what I want to know is how are you going to get my son to stop going around and around in a circle with the horse? He loves repetitive activities."

"Well," Whitney said as she rubbed her chin, trying to come up with something that would work, "let me try this."

She strode to Jason and fell into step with him, grabbing the reins where she'd held them before. The child didn't falter. He kept going even when she directed them toward the barn.

"I'm impressed. You have a way with my son," Shane whispered close to her ear.

The feel of his breath on her neck made her shiver. She shouldn't have asked them to stay. Why had she? She was afraid to answer that question.

She led Big Red into his stall, motioned for Shane to bring the mutt near, then distracted Jason with the dog. Quickly she rounded up the kids who had ridden with her and Jason and headed across the field toward the cluster of cottages and one large two-story house set slightly apart from them.

"What did Peter say about the dog?" Whitney asked halfway across the meadow, all the children, including Jason and the mutt, twenty yards ahead of them.

"He's going to gift wrap him with a big red bow for us."

"Did you tell him to make that a big yellow bow?"

Shane's laughter sprinkled the air, causing a couple of the kids to glance back at them and giggle. "So you come out here every Sunday and go riding with the some of the children. Do you volunteer any other times?"

"Sometimes I come on Saturday afternoon, too.

Until I started taking some classes at the university, I also came out here at least three evenings. I've had to cut that back to one." And she missed the kids. She looked into some of their faces and saw glimpses of herself before she'd become so jaded. She was determined they wouldn't have a life like hers.

"You're a busy lady."

"It feels right to work with the kids."

"The Lord has it right. It's better to give than receive."

She thought about that and nodded. "Yeah, it is. The smiles on their faces make me forget my worries."

"What worries? It sounds like you've got things figured out."

She bit back a snort and hurried her pace. "We'd better catch up with the kids."

Andy glimpsed an old Chevy car and ran ahead. "Mom's here."

One of the housemothers came out on the porch of the nearest cottage. "I was just about to send the cavalry to get you all." She gestured toward three of the children. "You all need to wash up. Dinner is in fifteen minutes. Are you eating with us tonight, Whitney?"

"Not tonight. I'm here for Hannah's spaghetti."

"It's nice seeing you out here, Dr. McCoy." The

woman waved goodbye as she took up the rear while the kids filed into the house.

"I'd better go," Shane said as the front door of the two-story house opened. "We'll need to grab something—"

"Shane, what a surprise to see you here." Hannah descended the steps and crossed her yard. "And you brought Jason. I gather he's been to the barn. You've got Barney." She pointed at the dog.

"Yeah, Peter gave us the dog. So his name is Barney?"

"As of yesterday, one of the young children named him after that cartoon character on TV, but he doesn't come to it so name him whatever you want."

Kneeling in front of his son, Shane waited until Jason looked at him. "Do you like the name Barney for him?" He patted the mutt who had to be a mix of several large breeds from a black Lab to a boxer.

"Doggie."

"Yes, he's a dog, but do you want to call him Barney?"

"Doggie." Jason stomped his foot.

"I think he likes the name Doggie." Whitney chuckled at the perplexed expression on Shane's face.

"I hope you two can join us for spaghetti

tonight." Hannah strolled toward the porch. "I have plenty. Jacob took our sons out camping this weekend, and he called to say they were running late, that he'd grab something for them to eat on the road back here. So it's just us girls and Andy, who I'm sure would love some male company."

"I should get home since tomorrow will be Jason's first full day at school, but there's no way I'm turning down my son's favorite dinner."

"We are ready to eat at any time, so you two should be able to get home at a decent hour." Hannah stepped to the side to allow them to enter her house first.

When Jason moved forward with Doggie in tow, Shane stopped him with a hand on his shoulder. "We need to leave your dog out on the porch."

Hannah waved her hand. "Oh, don't worry about your pet. You should see the ones my kids have. Sometimes I think I'm running a zoo here." Stooping to eye level, she waited until Jason gave her his attention. "Let's go find Andy. I believe he made a mad dash for the playroom in back." She rose. "You two go on into the den. We'll have some adult time before dinner. I'll take care of Jason getting settled with the others."

"But I'd better—"

Whitney grasped Shane's arm to still his words. "Is Lisa in the den?"

"Yep." Hannah escorted Shane's son and new pet toward the back.

"You don't understand. Jason might—"

"Act a little differently? That's okay. You can't always protect him." At one time in her life, Whitney would have given anything for her father to show any kind of concern for her.

"It isn't necessarily him but the others. My son can throw a tantrum when things get too much for him to handle."

"Andy's a wonderful kid. He'll come get us if that happens. Don't worry."

Whitney found Lisa in the den. "Andy told me the good news."

"He did?" With a look of disappointment, the tall, young woman with short white-blond hair rose and engulfed Whitney in a hug. "I should have known he would say something. He can never keep a secret."

Whitney pulled back. "Secret? I'd be shouting it at the top of my lungs. Getting your high school diploma is a big deal."

Lisa's blue eyes brightened. "Yes, it is, and yesterday your brother promoted me to manager because I have it now. He told me he was just waiting for me to finish my online course work. I'm the manager of his number one restaurant!"

"I can't believe my brother kept that from me.

I'll have to have a word with Noah." Whitney turned toward Shane. "This is Lisa Morgan, the new manager at The Ultimate Pizzeria." She swept her arm toward him. "Lisa, Dr. Shane McCoy."

"Oh, yes, I've seen you in the restaurant." The twenty-six-year-old stepped toward him and shook his offered hand. "Tonight we have some celebrating to do. And I can't think of any other people besides you and Hannah that I want to do that with."

"Congratulations, Lisa." Shane sat in the chair nearest the entrance into the den.

Whitney took the one across from him. "So does Jason like pizza?" She peered at her friend. "Lisa, Jason is Shane's son."

"That is his other food he likes at dinner. We've had a lot of your brother's pizza at my house."

"If my memory serves me right, you come in at least three times a week for carryout. You should come and dine in one evening." Lisa reclaimed her seat on the couch.

A frown touched the corners of his mouth. "It's usually better if I take it home."

"Jason might like the games and rides that Noah has added to that store. Most kids don't want to leave."

Shane pinned her with an unreadable look. "Jason isn't most kids."

As Hannah returned to the den, Whitney

relaxed back in her chair and watched Shane talk with both women. Although he said all the right things, she sensed his attention was only partially on the conversation flowing around him. She didn't know much about autism, but wasn't he being overprotective with his son?

Later that evening Shane pulled his SUV into Zoey's driveway and parked in front of the garage. After glancing at his son, who'd fallen asleep hugging his new dog, he pushed open his door and exited the vehicle.

Whitney locked her VW and approached him. "Satisfied? I'm home safe and sound."

"You can never be too careful."

She leaned close and lowered her voice. "You can rest easy now."

He grinned. "Not until I see you safely inside."

"Guess what? I've been taking care of myself for twenty-eight years. I think I can walk up those stairs without anything going wrong."

He did get the distinct impression she had been the one who had seen to her own care, even as a child. "Humor me."

She shrugged and proceeded toward the staircase that led to her apartment, mumbling something about where she came from chivalry had gone the way of the eight-track tape. Shane followed her.

Halfway up Whitney tripped on the step and nearly went to her knees if Shane hadn't caught her. When he brought her back against him, her citrus scent enveloped him like an embrace. He immediately pulled away, dropping his arms to his sides.

She glanced over her shoulder at him, a baffled look in her eyes. Quickly she mounted the rest of the stairs and fumbled in her purse until she withdrew her key.

Suddenly he didn't want the evening to end. He'd enjoyed himself after all that had happened that day—all because of the woman standing in front of him. "Thanks for talking me into staying for dinner at Hannah's. You're right. Her spaghetti is delicious. Jason doesn't usually eat all his dinner, but he cleaned his plate."

"He beat everyone which is quite a feat since Andy can shovel it into his mouth."

"I was amazed at how Andy looked after Jason and how my son let him."

"Although Andy doesn't live at the refuge anymore, he's there a lot. I think he loves animals as much as your son."

"Yeah, he was already showing Jason a trick to teach Doggie." Shane leaned back against the wooden railing and gripped it on each side. "I can't believe Jason wants to call his pet *Doggie.*"

"I knew someone who called her cat *Cat,*"

Whitney said with a chuckle. "How's your aunt going to feel about having a dog in the house?"

"She has mentioned getting a pet to me a few times lately, so she'll be fine with it."

"When do you pick her up at the hospital?"

"Knowing Aunt Louise, right after I drop Jason off at school."

"What happens if you can't leave him?"

He smiled. "I think the Lord sent you to help me. Jason has bonded with you quickly, and I think there's a reason for that."

"Not my winning personality and good looks?" Whitney jiggled the keys in her hand.

"Although you have both, there's something about you that my son responds to. Personally I think he's a good judge of character, just on a different level." The sound of the clanking keys increased as she stared at a spot to the left of him. "Are you okay with escorting him into the building tomorrow?"

Her wide gaze swept back to him. "I don't understand what's going on with Jason, but I certainly know what it is like to be different."

"Maybe he senses that." He pushed away from the railing. "I don't really understand everything going on with my son, either. He looks at life through a blurry windshield. The wipers will never completely clear away the rain obscuring his view."

She stopped her jiggling and clutched her keys. "That's an interesting way to look at your child."

Even though darkness crept over the landscape, only a few feet separated Whitney from him, and there was enough light to see a tug-of-war of emotions cross her face. Her hand about the keys strengthened its grasp, her knuckles white.

"What time will you be bringing Jason?"

"I'm flexible." He gave a short laugh. "I have to be with my son. Tell me what the best time for you would be, and I'll try to accommodate."

"Why don't we try right after school starts? That way all the other kids will be in class. Less confusion for Jason to handle."

"I like that suggestion. I'll be there at eight-thirty then."

She pivoted to unlock her door.

He laid his hand on her shoulder to catch her attention and tell her thanks again. She fumbled the keys, and they fell to the planked floor. He bent over to pick them up at the same time she did. Their gazes met—only inches between them. Her eyes grew round. She snatched up the keys and bolted to an erect stance.

"See you tomorrow morning." Quickly she slipped inside her apartment.

He moved to leave, hesitated and stared back at the door. Whitney Maxwell stirred something in him. Perhaps it was his son's fondness for her that heightened his awareness of the woman, but he was afraid it was much more. And that could not be. He'd given his heart to his wife years ago. He didn't have anything left for someone else.

He hurried down the stairs to his SUV. As he opened his door, he glanced up at Whitney's apartment and saw her staring out the window at him. He waved goodbye.

Whitney turned away, her arms glued to her sides. Leaning back against the wall, she finally heard his car leave and slumped to the floor. When they had been talking about why Jason responded to her, she couldn't help thinking the reason was he sensed how she had been abandoned, still felt that way even though her brother had done his best to change that. She didn't understand where that thought had come from. Was that also why she and the children at the refuge got along so well, not to mention Peter, who collected every abandoned animal he could find?

She clenched her hands. Anger wormed its way into her. She didn't like what was happening. Her life was changing too fast. She had no control over it anymore. She needed that control to make her life work.

Noah had told her to put her trust in the Lord.

It appeared as though Shane did. Was that the answer? She just didn't see that. She didn't trust anyone completely, most people not at all. That ability had been destroyed with each blow her father had landed on her, when her adopted parents had only wanted someone to do all the work for them and used force to get what they wanted, and when she'd lived on the streets as a fifteen year old. Freezing. Hungry. Desperate.

She buried her face against her raised knees. No, the Lord would never forgive her for what she'd done to survive those first few months on her own. She'd accepted she was damaged goods and would have to go through life alone.

But the hurt she wished she could deny burrowed deep into her heart.

Chapter Five

While waiting on the sidewalk for Jason to show up for what would hopefully be his first full day of school, Whitney cradled the brown rabbit in her arms. When she'd asked Mrs. Bradley if she could bring the class pet when she picked up Jason, the woman had said yes but had immediately launched into her usual spiel about how the child probably wouldn't flourish in a regular classroom. Whitney's own doubt rose as she listened to Jason's teacher talk. If the educator didn't support Jason being in the room, it would be hard for there to be any success.

The sound of the bell blasted the morning quiet, announcing the start of school. At that moment Shane drove into the oval driveway and parked his SUV. At first Jason wouldn't leave the car. But when he glimpsed Whitney with the rabbit, he jumped from the SUV and charged toward her, oblivious to any cars coming toward him.

Looking both ways, she hurried forward into the lane, relieved that the one vehicle in the parking lot was heading toward the exit at the far end. She peered toward Shane, who had grabbed for his son and missed. His pale face filled her vision before she quickly turned her attention to the child skidding to a stop right in front of her. The tips of his shoes touched hers.

Jason planted his fingers into the brown fur, gently stroking the animal. "Hop. Hop."

While Shane approached, slowing his pace when he saw she had his son, Whitney drew the boy to the sidewalk. "Yes, a rabbit hops around. Would you like to hold Cottontail?"

"I've been working with him about crossing streets." Shane ruffled his son's hair. "Obviously we need to work more on it."

Whitney placed the class pet in Jason's outstretched arms. He immediately pulled it against his chest and rubbed his cheek across the fur. "Next time why don't you pull up to the curb?"

"That can only work if I don't have to park to bring Jason into the building."

"I have confidence this will work."

"I hope. Aunt Louise called me as I was leaving. She's ready to come home."

Whitney drew closer to Shane and whispered, "If I can get him into the classroom and taking care of the rabbit, leave."

"He might do fine with the rabbit, but what about later?"

"Don't worry. There's always a period of adjustment for everyone, not just Jason. There comes a time when you need to leave him. Don't you think it's better if we don't get him too used to you being in the classroom with him?"

He chuckled. "That's a good point. I certainly don't want to be attending kindergarten again. I don't fit in the small chairs."

"Then we've got a game plan. Here goes." She shifted back to the child. "Jason, do you want to see where Cottontail lives?" As she had seen Shane do, Whitney settled her hand on his shoulder to guide him toward the door.

The boy didn't reply, but when she moved toward the double doors into the building, he didn't resist. Inside he continued with Whitney to his kindergarten class, not once looking back to see if his father was there.

Shane trailed behind them. At the door she mouthed the words "Stay back," then entered the room with Jason focused totally on the animal in his arms.

She'd gotten the teacher's permission to let

Jason feed the rabbit and fill its water bottle that hung on the side of the large cage. He went through the routine without any problems and let her place Cottontail in his cage. Whitney signaled to Shane to leave. He hesitated for a few seconds, then disappeared from the doorway.

She knew the real test would be when Jason had to leave the rabbit. Inhaling a fortifying breath, Whitney took his hand and guided him to a table where some of his classmates already were seated and working. Earlier she'd put a yellow can of crayons in front of his place, hoping that would draw him to his chair.

He didn't see the can. Instead, his attention latched on to the boy in the chair next to his. Jason wrenched free and fled. The teacher moved to block the doorway into the hall. Jason saw her, then veered to the right, making a beeline for the large yellow ball in the corner, not far from the rabbit's cage. He fell on the ball, hugging it even though it was too big to get a good grip.

Whitney started for Jason, then stopped and looked toward Mrs. Bradley in case she wanted to handle the situation. The older woman nodded for her to go on and deal with the child while she stepped away from the door to handle another incident with three girls by the reading circle.

Whitney went back to the table, retrieved

Jason's crayons in the yellow can, some white paper and two clipboards. Amanda, Mrs. Bradley's regular teacher's assistant, stood on the other side, hovering near two children who had been acting up earlier. She leaned over one and pointed at something on the paper the little girl was writing on. Amanda's long-sleeved shirt rode up on her arm a couple of inches and for a few seconds revealed several fingertip-sized bruises right above her wrist. That sight piqued Whitney's concern. Those bruises instantly brought forward a memory she usually kept buried. Had someone physically tried to restrain Amanda? Her boyfriend? She looked away, not wanting the young woman to see her staring, but she frowned at the possible implications.

Amanda snagged her attention. "Is everything okay with the little boy?"

"Yeah, he just needs some time to adjust." At least he wasn't throwing a tantrum, Whitney thought and smiled at Amanda before moving away from the table.

She would keep an eye on the young woman and see if there were any other signs of being abused. Maybe that boyfriend wasn't Mr. Wonderful, the term Amanda had called him one day at lunch.

When Whitney sat cross-legged on the floor next to Jason, she began drawing on one of the pieces of paper. At first he didn't pay attention to her, but slowly he stopped hugging the ball and stared at what she was doing.

When a picture of the rabbit appeared on the paper, he came to her side and pointed at it. "Hop. Hop."

"Yes, that's Cottontail."

"Cotton—tail." He dug into the yellow can, pulled out a brown crayon and bent over the other clipboard with paper.

While Jason worked, Mrs. Bradley came over. "I'm sending Amanda to take your place in Miss Robertson's room. At least for the day. We may have to look at a permanent move."

"Okay." Whitney had enjoyed working with the children in Miss Robertson's class. Mrs. Bradley and she didn't see eye to eye on things. She wasn't sure how she felt about moving to this classroom.

That feeling was reconfirmed throughout the day, and when she met with the principal at the end of the day, she wanted to tell the woman that she would prefer staying in Miss Robertson's class. But Whitney couldn't say the words.

"So my primary job will be to work with Jason in Mrs. Bradley's class?" Whitney asked, sitting in front of the principal's desk.

"Yes. I'm leaving Amanda in there, too, at

least until we find out if this situation will work for Jason."

Whitney wanted to ask what would happen if it didn't. Would they insist that Jason move to a different setting, possibly at another school that the district felt was more appropriate? Shane wanted his son at his home school. He wanted him with children in the regular education classroom. But would that work?

When Whitney left the principal's office, she made her way to the parking lot. The sun beat down upon her. In her car she cranked up the air-conditioning, hoping the interior would cool off quickly. As she drove toward the university where she would begin a new class in an hour, she decided to go to the library and check out a book about autism.

At the first corner, Whitney saw Amanda heading down a side street. She made a U-turn and went in the direction the young woman was going.

Whitney slowed and pulled up slightly ahead of Amanda. "Hop in. I can give you a ride home."

Dressed in long pants and shirt, sweat coating her face, Amanda hesitated, glancing around her as though checking to see if anyone was watching. "I need the exercise. I've been putting on weight."

Putting on weight? Amanda was reed thin. "I was hoping you would give me your take on how today went with Jason."

"You want my opinion?"

"Sure. You work well with the children. Hop in."

Again Amanda peered up and down the street, nibbling on her lip, then strode toward the passenger's side. "I think he's adorable, and he sure has taken to you," she said as she slipped into the seat.

Whitney directed most of the vents blasting cold air toward Amanda. "Adorable and stubborn. He wrote his name today and wanted me to read a book about animals to him at least six times. The last time he said the words before I did. I think he had the whole book memorized already."

"Amazing."

"Yeah, I'm finding he is quite an amazing young man." Whitney stopped at a street intersection. "Where do you live?"

"You can drop me off at the end of the next block."

"Is this your first year working for Mrs. Bradley?"

"Yes. The teacher I was with last year retired. Mrs. Bradley is very different from her."

"How so?"

Amanda dropped her head and stared at her hands twisting together in her lap. "Oh, just different."

"Any insight you have will be appreciated. I'm trying to figure out how to work with her."

Amanda remained silent.

"Maybe one day after school we can go get some coffee and discuss it."

"I usually have to get home right after work." Amanda gestured toward the corner. "You can drop me off here."

Coming to a stop, Whitney scanned the intersection with businesses on all four corners. "I have time before my class to take you to your door."

Amanda climbed out of the car, then leaned in. "Thanks. See you tomorrow."

Whitney made a left turn and watched through the rearview mirror as Amanda walked in the opposite direction. The slump to the young woman's shoulders screamed low self-esteem. She should know. She'd been there herself. In that moment Whitney vowed she would befriend Amanda and see if she could help her. Something definitely was wrong, and Whitney was pretty sure it involved Mr. Wonderful.

That evening when Whitney drove past Shane's house after her early class at the university, the lights blazed from the rooms at the front of the house. She popped in her mouth the last bite of the small pizza she'd gotten on her way home. The second story was dark like the approaching night. Was Jason asleep early? Louise?

She pulled into Zoey's driveway and parked her VW. She'd wanted to be in the classroom when Shane picked up Jason, but she'd been called to the office to speak with the principal ten minutes before the dismissal bell, so she wasn't sure how it had gone at the end. She should have asked Amanda when she gave her a ride home, but all she'd been able to focus on was the young woman and the abuse she suspected Amanda endured.

Leaving her books and purse in her car, Whitney locked the door and headed across the street. On Shane's porch, she inhaled deeply and rang the bell. A moment later the door swung open, and Shane greeted her with a smile.

"I'm glad you came. I've been full of questions about Jason's first day. Mrs. Bradley didn't have much to say, but she did say you stayed with Jason all day so I thought I'd pump you for some info. Give." He waved her into his foyer. "Let's go in the den. Jason is asleep at eight o'clock. A first in a long time by the way. What did you do? Exhaust him?"

Whitney followed Shane into the den. "Where's Louise?"

"In her room. Tired, too. I'm the only one who isn't."

"I'm gonna have to join Jason and Louise's rank. It's been a long day."

Shane took a seat on the couch. "Sit and tell me everything. All day I was waiting for a call from the school to come pick up my son."

Should she tell him about the tantrum on the

playground when Jason was supposed to go back into the classroom? Or about the negative vibes she'd received from Mrs. Bradley when Jason didn't do everything exactly like she'd planned?

She sat at the other end of the couch and shifted to face him, her arm along the top of the back cushion. "The reason I wasn't there when you came at the end of the day is because the principal wanted to talk to me about moving to Mrs. Bradley's room permanently. She wanted to make sure I was okay about it."

Both of his eyebrows rose. "And are you?"

No—yes. Somehow she would deal with the teacher because she had told the principal she would change. "Yes, Jason and I are doing fine."

"What aren't you telling me?"

"What makes you think that?"

"Your tone. I know my son. Something happened. What?"

"It really isn't me and Jason. He had one tantrum on the playground because he didn't want to leave the swing, but when I walked into the building with the yellow ball, he followed me to class. I never got him to sit at his table, but he did some work in the corner where the ball is kept. The rabbit cage isn't far, and when he finished one task, I let him hold the rabbit for five minutes. I used a timer and when it rang he would do the next task."

"But?"

While Jason had worked by himself, Mrs. Bradley had still insisted Whitney stay near him instead of helping some of the other children, even ones nearby—as though she were the boy's bodyguard, there to keep others away, even Mrs. Bradley who hadn't interacted with him at all. Whitney peered down at her lap, not sure how to express her mixed feelings about the situation she found herself in. "I'm just a little frustrated with the teacher, but it's only the first day working with her."

"Why are you frustrated?"

"Don't go into your counseling mode, Dr. McCoy. I'll work my problems out with Mrs. Bradley."

"I see. Do these problems have to do with Jason?"

"Not really."

"But some?"

Exasperated, she blew out a breath of air. "You don't give up, do you?"

"I want this to work for my son, but I don't want it to cause you any problems. Jason has formed a bond with you that I can't ignore, but I have a feeling you were moved to a situation that isn't to your liking. I can talk with the principal and get you moved back to your original classroom."

Anger welled up in her. She shot to her feet. "Don't you dare. I enjoy working with Jason. I fight my own battles. If I want to be moved back, I'll go to the principal. Mrs. Bradley and I will work it out."

"Fine. You've made yourself perfectly clear. But you don't have to fight all 'your battles' as you put it by yourself. There are people in your life who would like to help as you are helping them." Shane pointed to his chest. "I'm one of them."

"I like to help others."

He stood and strode to her, his intense gaze fixed on hers. "So do I."

Her anger dissolved as quickly as it flared. She was tired and frustrated, but Shane wasn't responsible. Neither was Jason. She was concerned about Mrs. Bradley being the right teacher for Jason. And she was worried about Amanda, afraid she was going through what she had when she was eighteen. "I don't always play well with others. I'm—sorry," she managed to say although apologizing to someone was hard for her.

The corner of his mouth lifted. "And I'm sorry, too. I was being, as you told me once, *relentless.* I'll try not to be in the future."

The way he'd said *future* made it sound as if there was a future for her and Shane. And she guessed there was since she would be working with his son. Not the future she had been planning.

He held out his hand. "Friends?"

She looked at it for a few seconds then fit her hand in his. "Friends." That was all it could be. She had a plan and it did not include a relationship beyond friendship.

"Would you like something to drink?"

She shook her head. "I need to be going, but I wanted to let you know about Jason's first day and say hi to Louise if she's still up."

"Let me go check. She was reading her Bible the last time I saw her."

When Shane left the den, she took a moment to inspect the room. The only other time she'd been in his house was that first day a week ago. Everything in the maroon and navy room matched down to the throw pillows. It was neat and orderly from the magazines stacked on the coffee table to the basket of toys in the corner, none scattered about the floor as they were in Noah's house. Yep, just as she thought, it was most likely Shane's doing, not his aunt's, since she had been in the hospital or resting in her room for the past day and a half.

Shane appeared in the doorway. "Aunt Louise would love to see you. She'd heard the bell and us talking and was going to come in and see you."

"Great, this saves her a trip." She passed him and headed toward the room he indicated.

He didn't follow.

The door was open so she strolled into the bedroom and found the older woman sitting up in bed, her Bible in her lap. A smile spread across her face as Whitney approached, welcoming her with a warmth she had rarely encountered. For a brief moment she wondered what it would have been like to have a loving mother as she'd grown up.

"I'm so glad you didn't leave before seeing me."

After scooting a chair closer to Louise, Whitney sat. "How are you doing?"

"Tired. The doctor insists that I slow down, but he doesn't realize I have an active six-year-old to keep up with. In order to get Jason in school, Shane has cut back meeting with his patients this past week, and now I can't do all I need to do. He often meets with the children he counsels in the late afternoons and into the evenings. Also, he works on most Saturdays, at least part of the day. He was home all day today, hovering. He didn't even want me to get a glass of water by myself. He needs to get back to work full-time before I kill him," Louise said with a laugh.

"I can help you on the weekends and on those evenings I don't have a class after school."

"You're going to school?"

"Yeah, I'm taking two classes, one's on Monday right after work. It started this week. The other is on Thursday from seven to nine. Otherwise, I'm available to help when you need it." If she had to, she could rearrange her volunteer time at Stone's Refuge, at least until Louise was her old self again.

"When are you going to study, child?"

"Don't you worry about that. There'll be time." Whitney leaned close and lowered her voice. "Just so you know, I don't do *hovering*."

Louise's laughter filled the air. "That's comforting to know."

Whitney rose. "Then it's settled. I'll be over after school and if you need me, I'll stay."

"Child, that's the best news. Shane is so worried he'll lose me like his wife."

Whitney was tempted to ask more questions about Shane's wife and the type of relationship they'd had, but she kept her mouth shut. It really didn't take a brain surgeon to figure out the man was still deeply in love with his deceased wife. Wearing his wedding ring after five years screamed that to the world.

"Good night." Whitney squeezed Louise's hand gently then strode from the bedroom.

She found Shane in the kitchen off the den, rinsing some plates and glasses and putting them into the dishwasher. When she entered, he looked up.

"Just wanted to tell you I'm leaving."

He shut the door on the appliance and switched it on. "Let me walk you home."

She put her hands on her waist. "I can walk home by myself. I walked here by myself." She twirled around. "And look, I'm okay."

"I know but I could use the exercise and fresh air."

"Are you manipulating me into agreeing?"

"Is it working?" He advanced toward her, a smile dimpling his cheek. "Honestly, I do need to get out of the house."

"Come on then." She swung around and made her way to the front door.

Outside darkness totally enveloped the neighborhood except the occasional house light and the lone streetlamp at the end of the block. A sweet scent perfumed the light breeze. Crickets chirped. An owl hooted in the distance. Tranquil. Light years away from her old life in Dallas or, for that matter, any of the other places she'd lived before coming back to Cimarron City.

Shane took a deep breath. "Ah, peace. I love this time of day."

Whitney descended the porch steps. "I told Louise I would come over after work tomorrow and help her. Now that I think about it, I would like to bring Jason home from school. That would save you or Louise from having to pick him up. I imagine you could use that time with your patients."

"I can't ask you to do that."

"First, you didn't. Second, weren't you the person who said it was okay to accept help?"

"Yeah, but I was talking about you, and you've already done enough for us."

"So there's a limit to the amount of help you can give a person?"

"Well, no, but the street should go both ways."

"I scratch your back and you'll scratch mine?"

He chuckled. "I don't know. Does it need scratching?"

She stopped on the sidewalk in front of Zoey's house and rounded on Shane, illuminated by a light on the lawn nearby. "You know exactly what I meant, Dr. McCoy."

His chuckles evolved into full laughter. "I know when I'm in trouble. I get the 'Dr. McCoy' treatment."

"Are you going to accept my help or not?" she asked in a mockingly stern voice.

"On one condition."

The merriment on his face erased his tired lines, sparking a response in Whitney she hurriedly squelched before she did something foolish like touch him. "What?"

"You let me take you out for dinner one evening when Louise is feeling better as my way of thanking you."

"A date?"

His eyes widened. "No, I don't date."

"Why not? Where I came from you'd be a prime catch."

His eyes grew even rounder. "*A prime catch!* I have a son with autism. Most women run the other way."

"They just haven't gotten to know Jason."

"Do you want it to be a date?"

"Oh, no. I don't date."

"Why not?"

"I have a plan, and it doesn't include a romantic involvement."

Rubbing the back of his neck, he shook his head. "How did we get on this conversation in the first place?"

"You asked me to dinner, and I wanted to make sure I wasn't reading it wrong, that we're just friends."

He moved his hand to his temple and massaged it. "My head is spinning. Are we going out to dinner or not?"

"Yes, when Louise is feeling better." Whitney spun on her heel and started down the driveway toward her apartment. "I'm glad we got our—relationship settled." At her car she unlocked it and retrieved her books and purse. "So I'll bring Jason home from school tomorrow, and you don't need to worry about a thing." She flashed him a smile and mounted the stairs.

His head positively ached from the short conversation he'd just had with Whitney. Shane strode back toward his house, welcoming the warm darkness about him. He certainly didn't want his neighbors to see the confusion and, yes, panic on his face. He was a man who kept a tight rein on his life, and at this moment he felt as though he had been in the middle of a whirlwind and hadn't fared well.

He'd simply wanted to thank her, not date her. He'd meant it. He didn't date. But why didn't she? She was single and from what he knew had never been married. She was beautiful, and although she sometimes hid behind a tough exterior, she wasn't really tough. She just wanted the world to think that.

Taking the steps to his porch two at a time, he hurried inside, no longer tired from the past week's activities. He would never have asked Whitney to help out while his aunt was recovering, but now that she was, he was pleased she'd volunteered. Jason liked her and that counted for a lot in his book.

Then why isn't your dinner a date?

That question came unbidden into his mind and halted his progress down the upstairs hallway.

You're unattached. She's unattached.

He shook his head to rid his mind of the thought and opened the door to his bedroom. His gaze immediately zeroed in on the framed photograph on his bedside table. Becka. That was the reason he didn't date.

How could he date? He was the reason she was dead.

Chapter Six

After school on Friday, Whitney pulled up to the curb in front of Shane's place, and before she'd turned off the engine, Jason released the clasp on his seat belt, slammed the car door open and raced toward his house. On Tuesday, the first day she'd brought the child home, she'd scrambled quickly after him, not sure what he was up to. Thankfully now she didn't have to move quite so fast because exhaustion clung to her like an extra set of clothing. Working with Jason this past week at school and at his home had been fulfilling—and tiring.

And her concern for Amanda had grown the more she had been around the young woman. One day Amanda had moaned when she had risen from sitting on the floor working with a group of children. Today she'd limped slightly. Both times she had dismissed Whitney's concerns. Amanda had told her that she was accident-prone and needed to be more careful. But Whitney knew what was happening. Her earlier vow to help had been reconfirmed all week while she watched and listened to the young woman. Worry for her new friend weighed on her mind. Whitney trudged toward the porch.

Louise opened the door before she reached the final step. "I figured you weren't too far behind him." The older woman scrutinized Whitney. "Child, come in and sit. In fact, even better, go home and take a nap."

"If I took a nap, I'd be up all night." She moved into the house, its coolness a welcome respite. "Besides, I'm here. I might as well stay for a while."

"You just want to see if Jason finally taught Doggie to rollover."

"Did he?"

"Come look for yourself. Jason sped through the house and out back so fast I wasn't sure who had opened and closed the back door." Louise raised the blinds in the kitchen nook and waved Whitney into the chair in front of the bay window. "It looks like you could use a tall iced tea."

"Mmm. You make the best tea. I've been thinking about it all day. Care to share your secret?"

Louise pulled a pitcher out of the refrigerator and withdrew two glasses from the cabinet.

"Maybe one day. This way you'll keep coming back for more." After easing down into the chair across from Whitney, Louise poured the tea.

Whitney took her drink, and while sipping it, observed Jason go through the tricks he'd taught Doggie every afternoon after school. After his pet had finished rolling over, Jason pulled out a hula hoop and started to teach Doggie to jump through it.

"I think watching Animal Planet has given him ideas." Whitney turned back to Louise.

"How's school going?"

"He's amazing. Today he was adding and even subtracting while the other children were working on counting. And when he drew a picture of Doggie, it was beautiful. Mrs. Bradley is even displaying it in the hallway."

"There's a lot to the boy. I've noticed just in this past week he's been talking more."

"He still isn't talking much at school, and only to me. We've moved his place to the corner where he feels most comfortable. But I still want him to sit at the table with some of the other children at least for some of his work."

"How are you and Mrs. Bradley getting along?"

Whitney sat up straight. "Did Shane say something about that to you?"

The older woman crunched her eyebrows

together. "No, but he did mention he was going to keep an eye on the teacher. He wasn't sure she was the one to teach Jason. Why? Are you having trouble with Mrs. Bradley?"

"Not trouble exactly." She relaxed again, the tension siphoning from her. "We just don't see things the same."

"Especially when it comes to Jason?"

She nodded. "I finally got her to interact with Jason today when I showed her how he was adding and subtracting in his head. She was amazed."

"Interesting the talents the Lord has given Jason. Just like he's given you a talent to work with children. I'm glad you're studying to be a teacher. You have a gift. Did you know when Jason says his prayers at night he's added your name to the list of people he wants God to watch over?"

The news stunned Whitney. "He has?" Her heart overflowed with an emotion she was afraid to acknowledge—love. Anytime she had cared for someone, that person had been snatched from her—her brother, several childhood friends and even her mother who had run away because of her father. She'd never had a chance with her mother.

"Most definitely. You're right after Shane and me and before Doggie. That says a lot."

Whitney swallowed several times, but the tightness in her throat wouldn't go away. Taking a long sip of her iced tea, she averted her gaze before Louise read the feelings she wrestled with.

Silence lingered in the kitchen, only broken by the ticking sound of the clock on the wall.

Whitney took a deep breath. A faint odor of lemon polish hung in the air. "You haven't been housecleaning, have you?"

"I'd better get Jason in. I need to start dinner." Pushing herself to her feet, Louise rose. "It'll feel good to cook again. I told Shane not to bring anything home because I was going to fix dinner. He protested, but I told him cooking was a stress reliever for me."

"Louise, you didn't answer my question. Are you overdoing it?"

"I'm not one to sit still for long. What kind of life do I have if I can't do for the ones I love? So yes, I did a few things around the house." The older woman challenged her with a look.

"And here I thought it was Shane who cleaned the house so spotless. I was thinking of hiring him to do my apartment. I hate to clean," Whitney said to interject some humor into the suddenly tense moment.

Louise sighed, her stiff stance wilting some. "I'm sorry to snap at you, but I've already been through this with Shane. He's wants me to sit around, watching soaps all day and eating bonbons."

Whitney laughed. "He said that?"

"Well, not exactly in those words, but that was the gist of his meaning." Shane's aunt took the pitcher of tea and stuck it back into the refrigerator. "Do you want to stay for dinner? I always make plenty."

"Oh, no. I still have boxes to unpack. I promised myself I would finish this weekend so I need to start." Whitney stood, downing the last of her tea. "But you go on and start. I'll watch Jason outside for you."

"You don't have—"

"Remember that's why I'm here. To help. Besides, sitting in the grass under the tree isn't what I consider exhausting work."

When Whitney stepped out into the backyard, Jason ran over to her and dragged her where Doggie was patiently waiting for him.

"Watch, Whitney."

With a huge grin on his face, he demonstrated how his pet could jump through the hoop. Again emotions jammed her throat as she thought of this little boy praying to the Lord on her behalf. Other than her brother, she'd never known of another doing that. The gesture awed her beyond words.

"How long have they been outside?" Shane asked Louise when he came home from work.

"An hour. Jason went from having Doggie jump through a hoop while standing on the ground to doing it from the porch. Now I think he's setting up some kind of obstacle course."

"When's dinner?"

"Half an hour."

Shane sniffed the air. The scent of a roasting chicken, onions and spices swirled around him. "I'm starved and that smells wonderful."

"I'm hoping that Jason will try some, but if he doesn't want it, I have slices of pizza leftover from last night."

"He doesn't know what he's missing with your cooking. I'll bring him in soon."

Shane turned from his aunt's beaming smile to peer out the bay window. Whitney pointed to a small table on the back porch. Jason raced to it and hauled it over to his quickly developing obstacle course. Then she helped him set it up. When they finished, Jason threw his arms around Whitney. She hugged him back. His son remained glued to her. She combed her fingers through his hair a few times then knelt in front of Jason, saying something to him. His son smiled from ear to ear and nodded.

Jason didn't interact with many people. *Why Whitney? And why, Lord, can't I get her out of my mind? Why do You keep throwing us together? What do You want me to do?*

All week he'd been perplexed by those questions. His life had gone back to a semblance of what it was once like—before Jason had started school and Louise had gotten sick—while Whitney had interrupted her plans to help him with his son as Louise regained her strength.

"You'd better get Jason, and maybe you can convince Whitney to stay for dinner." Aunt Louise opened the oven and removed the large baking dish.

Stepping outside, Shane immediately covered the distance to his son and Whitney, sitting on the grass with Doggie between them.

She looked up and rose. "You're home. I didn't realize it was that late. I'd better get going."

All week when he had come home from work Whitney had been gone, usually only ten or fifteen minutes before he arrived. "Have you been avoiding me?" he asked as Jason jumped up and raced toward the house.

She bent over and dusted off her pants.

"And are you avoiding me now?"

Rising up, she stared him in the eye. "Actually I don't have an answer for you. I'm not sure how to take you. You are so different from other—others I've known."

"Other men?"

"Yes. I know we talked about being friends, but frankly I haven't had a man as a friend before."

"How's that different from being friends with a woman?"

"It is, but I haven't had many friends who were women, either. I don't count Noah and his family or, for that matter, his extended family."

"What about Lisa and Hannah?"

"I meant before coming to Cimarron City. This is all new to me." She started walking toward the back door.

Interesting. Is this what You want me to do, Lord? Show Whitney how to be friends? "Being friends means doing things together, sharing. It's often not different from our close relationships with family members." He shrugged. "I really never thought about it."

"Sharing? Like what?"

"Sharing yourself—thoughts, hopes, dreams, what's bothering you."

"Oh, okay." She started to open the door but stopped midmotion. "I'm worried about someone I work with. I think she's being abused by her boyfriend."

"Why do you say that?"

"Woman's intuition?" She massaged her nape, rolling her shoulders as though that would ease the sudden tension he felt pouring off Whitney. "She wears clothes that aren't appropriate to the season—always long sleeves and pants, even when it's in the nineties and the children go outside for recess. I can see she's miserable and sweating a lot, but she doesn't change the type of clothes she's wearing. I took her home on Monday, and she wouldn't let me drop her off in front of her place. I saw bruises on her arm that looked like fingerprints on her skin. She's hurting and she chalks it up to being accident-prone. Something is going on."

"And you want to help." His admiration for Whitney went up a notch. "Be yourself. Engage her in a conversation and keep trying. I have confidence in you."

A blush tinted her cheeks.

"Don't you know you are a special lady? That's what Jason told me, and I agree one hundred percent."

Her eyes widened, the color leaching from her cheeks. She whirled around, wrenched open the door and escaped inside.

By the time he entered, she already had her purse and was digging in it for her keys. "Why don't you stay for dinner?"

Whitney glanced up from searching her large black leather bag. "Can't. I have things to do. See you all tomorrow."

She hurried from the kitchen, said something to Jason that Shane didn't hear and was gone before he could make it to the foyer. The sound of the front door closing announced her escape had been a success.

Right before she had come into the kitchen, he'd glimpsed panic in her eyes. When he had talked about how friends shared and later when he told her she was a special lady. The advice he'd given her about the woman at work was something he needed to heed in regard to Whitney. Her barriers were sky high, but he would continue to try and scale them—for his son's sake.

"Now don't get mad at me, but Aunt Louise insisted I bring this to you since you wouldn't stay for dinner." Shane held up a dish with a see-through lid that revealed some roasted chicken, rice and an assortment of cooked vegetables. "She thinks you won't stop and fix yourself anything to eat. She said something about you wanting to empty some of your boxes."

The crestfallen look he sent her produced a laugh. Whitney swung the door wide and let him in her apartment. "You can tell Louise I came right home and fixed a peanut butter and jelly sandwich. So I'm not starving."

"If you don't want me bringing you dinner every night, I'd better keep quiet what you ate tonight. Where do you want me to put this?"

"In the refrigerator. I'll eat it tomorrow night." Whitney stayed by the door, waiting for Shane to cross the room toward her. When he didn't but slowly made a full circle in the middle of her living room, she asked, "Is there something else?"

"I'm here to help you unpack."

"Louise's orders?"

"Nope. Mine." He raised his hand to cut off her protest. "You've been at my house helping all week, instead of unpacking your possessions. The least I could do is return the favor. That's what friends do for each other."

Friends. There was that word again. After his description of what he meant by sharing, she didn't know if she could even be friends with him. It just wasn't like her to reveal much about herself—at least not important stuff. Like her dreams and hopes. What she was feeling. What she'd gone through to get to this point.

"Maybe us being friends isn't such a good idea, Shane."

He faced her with that intense look he got when he had a point to make. "What are you scared about? Getting close to another person? Is it the 'sharing' part?"

She shut the door and took several steps toward him. "I don't trust people. Why would I share myself with others when they will only hurt me?"

"Because people are social and not meant to go through life alone. When God created Adam, He realized that and made Eve to keep Adam company."

"Yeah, and look what happened there. They were both kicked out of paradise."

"So you'd rather never experience the joys of a relationship, whether it is friendship or more, so you won't be hurt."

"Exactly."

"Chicken."

"I am not. I'm being practical."

Shane tossed back his head and laughed. "I haven't heard that one before. Well, for your information, Ms. Maxwell, you have shared something with me. You are afraid to trust anyone. You are not a risk taker, either."

"I am so."

"Yeah? What risk have you taken recently that involves your feelings?"

"Well," she said as she searched for an example, "Jason and I are friends."

"I mean with an adult."

"I—I—I'm sure there's one, but I'm so tired I can't seem to think straight."

He strode to her and lifted her chin so she looked him straight in the eyes. "Then go to bed early. Forget about unpacking tonight, and I'll be over here bright and early to help you. I don't have to go into the office until the afternoon. I'm at your service all morning. Good night."

After Shane left, Whitney collapsed into the nearest chair. Her mind was numb for a few seconds until thoughts flooded it. She should have asked him how early. She should have told him not to come. She should have kept her mouth shut from the very beginning. She was afraid he looked at her as a challenge, which sent alarms going off in her brain. A big mistake.

"Very good, Jason. You're holding the reins correctly." Whitney pulled hers to the right. "See how I can get Princess Leia to go exactly where I want? You try it."

When the boy mimicked her movements, a huge grin plastered his face. "I did it!"

"That's great, Jason."

She peered at Shane, who had just arrived and sat on the top rail of the paddock fence. She trotted her mare over to him.

"He loves riding." His grin rivaled his son's.

"Near the end of September there's going to be a big rodeo as a fund-raiser for Stone's Refuge downtown at the arena at Expo Square. A lot of the kids from here are going to participate in the rodeo. What do you think about Jason taking part with them?"

"But he's not a child at the refuge."

"Andy, as well as Noah's, Jacob's and Peter's children, are going to help. There'll be rodeo cowboys and clowns there, too. Some big names on the circuit have agreed to compete. It should be a lot of fun. I'm helping Peter organize the children's part in the show."

Shane's grip on the wooden slat tightened. "I don't know, Whitney. I think it would be too much for Jason."

"When I work with the others, can he participate? I'll never force him to do anything he doesn't want to or isn't safe for him."

"I know that. But I never know how my son is going to react in large crowds with a lot of noise. He can get overstimulated, then he'll shut down or throw a tantrum."

"He's a natural with the animals."

"Maybe he'll work in a zoo one day."

"I could see that. Or as an artist. Or a mathematician."

One of Shane's eyebrows arched. "A mathematician?"

"He's great with numbers."

"I know he was counting at an early age, but I never…" He stared at his son riding Big Red around and around the paddock, his attention totally focused on what he was doing.

"He has lots of possibilities."

"The sky's the limit?"

Whitney tilted her head to the side. "Don't you think so?"

"You do? Somehow I don't see you as an optimist."

"This isn't about me. This is about Jason." She needed the conversation centered on the child, not her. She was still recovering from their talk yesterday about friendship.

"Okay, I don't look at Jason through rose-colored glasses. He has limitations."

"We all have limitations. And I'm not looking through rose-colored glasses. No one that knows me well would say that."

"Who knows you well?"

"Ouch, that was a low blow. What's wrong?"

Shane slipped down from the railing, raking his hand through his hair. "It's nothing."

"It doesn't sound like it is."

"I feel like I'm losing a child I'm working with. Our session today didn't go well at all."

Whitney dismounted and tied the reins on the fence slat. "I'm sorry. That must be hard. Can you talk about it? That might help."

"Oh, you're good. It's okay if I talk about myself but not you. You steer me away from anything having to do with you. It's okay if you help me, but not the other way around. I came over to help you this morning, and you had to leave to go to the library to do some research for a paper. Friendship is a two-way street, and, right now, I'm feeling it's all one-way." He stalked out of the ring and headed into the barn.

Everything he said about her was dead-on. He'd called her a chicken the evening before, and she had realized she was. No wonder she didn't have many friends. It was hard work and scary.

"Jason," she said as she waited until the boy looked at her, then continued, "it's time to cool Big Red off."

She assisted him to the ground and watched him as he led the gelding around the maple tree. After she removed the riding equipment, Jason opened the gate to the pasture closest to them and let Big Red lose. In the barn Jason hurried to the sheep pen where Peter was inspecting a mother and her lamb.

"Is it okay if Jason joins you?" Whitney asked, wondering where Shane was.

"Yes." Peter showed Jason something Whitney couldn't see.

"I'll be back in a minute."

Whitney searched the area for Shane. When she didn't find him, she headed out front and spied him leaning back against the trunk of a huge oak, one foot propped against the tree while his hands were stuffed into his pockets. A frown marred his features.

She approached him, not sure what to say to him. That was her problem a lot of the time. She wasn't sure how to proceed.

Stopping in front of him, she waited until he looked at her. "I'm not good at this friend stuff. It comes naturally to people like Hannah, Peter, you, but not me. For the longest time I didn't think I had anything to give another person. When I discovered I did, I jumped in with both feet. I've discovered I like helping others. I'm still not comfortable, however, accepting help." She paused to catch her breath and to fortify her courage. "I'm sorry I left this morning. You're right. I panicked and ran. I'm good at that. I'd planned on unpacking when I returned home. Will you and Jason help me this evening?"

Stony silence hung in the air between them.

"No." He pushed himself away from the tree.

Chapter Seven

"Oh, okay," Whitney said, a catch to her voice she wished she could disguise. She swung around to head to the barn.

Shane halted her progress and turned her to face him. "I'll be over *without* Jason."

"But Jason is welcome to come."

"I know and that means a lot to me, but you use my son as a shield. If you really want to get this friendship thing down, then we need to spend time together without Jason. Do you have a problem with that? Do you want to rescind the invitation?"

She shook her head, the intensity pouring off Shane erasing all thoughts except ones centered on the man before her. Slightly rumpled, his hair tousled, he was different, as though he had come to some kind of decision.

He moved closer, his scent teasing her. "I don't

think you realize the extraordinary person you are," he said in a husky voice, cupping her cheek. "I meant what I said yesterday. I think you are a special lady."

His soft touch flowed through her as though mingling with her blood to infuse itself in her every pore. Robbed of coherent thought, all she could do was close her eyes and relish the feel of his skin against hers. He shifted even closer. Her lips tingled with anticipation.

Suddenly his hand fell away, leaving her bereft. Her eyes snapped open as he distanced himself.

"Remember, Whitney, special."

"Okay."

"I'd better get Jason and take him home before he wants to adopt another animal like a horse or sheep." He grinned. "I don't think my neighbors would appreciate that."

"Probably not," she murmured, watching him stride toward the barn's entrance.

What just happened here? That touch had nothing to do with being friends. What if more developed between— No! She couldn't think about or consider that. Love didn't exist for her. Maybe for others. But not her.

"When Noah called earlier, he told me to be sure and ask you, Jason and Louise to his second annual shindig to celebrate Labor Day." After removing the last of a set of dishes Cara insisted she take with her, Whitney stacked them in a cupboard.

"Who is coming to this shindig?" Shane opened the final box of kitchen items.

"Any adult or child connected with Stone's Refuge and a few additional friends. According to Cara, Noah went way overboard last year and intends to do the same thing this year. I imagine the children will enjoy it. Does Jason swim?"

"No. He's always been afraid of water. I took him to Lake Tenkiller once to fish, and he wouldn't get out of the car. A couple of times he's been near a pool and stays back, which frankly I'm glad about."

"Why?" She took the utensils he set on the counter and put them in the draw near the refrigerator.

"Because he has no sense of danger. I've been working with him on it, but still have a long way to go."

"Does he like to take a bath?"

"Loves it, but the larger the body of water, the more of a reaction I get from him."

Turning in the small kitchen to get the next set of utensils, she collided with Shane. "For one person this is fine, but any more makes it a little cramped."

"Probably where the saying 'too many cooks in the kitchen makes for a tight fit' comes from."

She laughed, her heart beating fast at his nearness. "I don't think that's how it goes, but it certainly applies here." Stepping away as far as she could in a one-person kitchen, she pointed to the last stack of boxes in the living room. "Go on and start with those. I'll be finished in a minute in here."

He threw a glance over his shoulder as he walked away. "I'm still wondering how you fed yourself when most of your kitchen stuff was packed away."

"How hard is it to make peanut butter and jelly? Besides, I knew where everything was and pulled it out if I needed it."

"That would have driven me crazy the first day." He held up sheets and two blankets. "Where do you want these?"

"Put them on my bed. I'll find a place for them later." When she completed putting up the kitchen items, she crossed to where Shane had opened the first of the last three boxes. Tossing the empty one in her growing pile, she tore into the second one.

When he reentered the living room, he eyed the cardboard boxes littering the floor by the entrance into the apartment. "Trying to hold me hostage here?"

The very idea heated her cheeks. Her heartbeat accelerated, and it took a moment for her to say, "That was the only place open to put the boxes." She cringed at the breathless quality to her voice.

"Tell you what, I'll break these down while you finish up with those last two."

"Ha! I wondered when you would say something about my little pile." She tamped down her reaction to the image that had popped into her mind at his comment earlier. *Strictly friends.*

"What's that supposed to mean?"

"You are a neat freak."

"And what's wrong with that? I don't spend wasted time looking for something because everything has a place in my house."

She swept around, hands on her waist. "Is that a snide reference to me hunting for my scissors earlier?"

"If the shoe fits…"

"Boy, you're just full of sayings this evening."

"Didn't you just tell me you knew where everything was in the boxes?"

"I meant the kitchen items."

"Oh."

She huffed as though exasperated with him, but as she turned back to work, a laugh escaped. When she slid a glance toward him to see if he heard it, she found him hidden behind the mound. Putting the books she had pulled out on the coffee table, she sneaked toward him to scare him.

Suddenly Shane shot up. She gasped, stumbling back. And down she went on her behind, so hard she lay sprawled on the carpet.

With boxes crashing everywhere, he fought his way toward her and knelt by her, hovering over her prone body. "Are you all right?"

She took one look at him and burst out laughing.

"What's so funny? I thought you might be hurt."

She reached up and yanked off the masking tape hanging from his shirt. "Nothing." Then she started laughing all over again, falling backward in her merriment.

Soon Shane joined her.

Tears ran down her cheeks. Finally she brushed them away and struggled to a sitting position, which put her dangerously close to Shane who had finally stopped laughing, too.

His gaze connected with hers. "Lesson one, shared laughter is part of being friends." He scrambled to his feet and took her hand, bringing her up almost against him. "See, the world as you know it didn't come to an end with me helping you up or, for that matter, with unpacking. Which leads me to lesson two, helping each other is another part."

Staring up into his eyes, she found herself

wanting to kiss Shane. Her gaze dropped to his mouth, and the lure was strong. She leaned slightly toward him.

Remember, strictly friends!

Thankfully common sense wrenched her out of the moment. As she shifted away, trying to bring some order to her hair, the ringing of her phone blared in the quiet.

Hurrying, she snatched it up and said, still a little breathless, "Hello."

"Whitney, this is Louise. Is Shane there?"

"Yes." The panic in the older woman's tone caused her own to mushroom. "Is something wrong?"

"Jason isn't in his bed. I was hoping he was over there or…" The woman's voice caught, losing momentum.

"We'll be right there."

Pale, Shane pivoted toward the door. "It's Jason, isn't it?"

She nodded. "She can't find him. He isn't in his bed."

"Maybe he's on his way over here."

She hoped so. Grabbing a flashlight, she hurried after Shane, running to catch up with his long strides as he headed down the driveway.

"Jason," he called out, scanning from side to side.

Whitney directed her light in the dark recesses

of night, praying the child was all right. That he hadn't somehow wandered off and gotten into trouble. With each step she took, her heart increased its beat until it was pounding against her chest when they arrived at Shane's.

Louise stood on the porch in a robe, her dark gray hair—usually pinned up—down about her shoulders. "I didn't set the alarm because you were gone. I retired to my room. I should have stayed in the den. I might have heard him leaving."

"You've checked everywhere in the house?"

"Twice."

"Does he run off often?"

"When Jason thinks of something, he acts without thinking. Time doesn't mean much to him. If he thought he should go to school, that's what he would do."

Shane stalked to his kitchen where he withdrew a heavy-duty flashlight and checked to make sure it worked before making his way back to the front door.

"Do you think he went to the school?"

He paused at the door, took a deep, calming breath and said, "I hope not. There are a lot of streets he would have to cross to get there. One major one and it's dark."

"What do you need me to do?" Whitney asked, picturing the child, running across four lanes of traffic without looking for oncoming cars. Her stomach knotted into a huge, hard ball.

"We'll check the neighborhood then go out from there."

"What do you want me to do, Shane?" his aunt asked, the tired lines of her face carved deep into her features.

"Stay here. He might come home." On the sidewalk Shane clicked on his flashlight. "I'll cover this direction. You go that way. Let's meet back here after we have gone several blocks."

With each step Whitney took away from the house, her fear inched higher. She couldn't imagine how Shane felt, his son missing, possibly in danger. Jason wasn't hers and a queasy, sickening sensation caused beads of sweat to blanket her face.

Thirty minutes later she returned to Shane's house empty-handed and mounted the steps to the porch to see if Louise had any news. She paused when she spotted Shane, a few houses away, his flashlight constantly sweeping the area, as he called out his son's name over and over, his tone frantic. A couple of the neighbors came out of their homes and stopped him along the way.

When he reached her, his haggard look tore at her. The dull flatness of his gaze settled on her face. "Nothing. Some people are coming to help us look. He's never been gone like this. I've always been able to find him. I can't…" He peered away, swallowing hard. "I can't lose another child. I can't, Whitney." A sheen glittered in his eyes.

Another child? He'd never said anything about losing a child until now. What other secrets had he kept to himself? He was more like her than she'd originally thought, and she of all people needed to respect his privacy. But it didn't stop her from wanting to know and realizing he didn't trust her enough to share his past with her.

She drew him into her embrace and held him for a moment. Each of his shudders went to her core, shaking her more than she thought possible. She wished she could absorb his pain and take it away.

She wasn't good at praying, wasn't even sure she knew how. But words welled up in her. *Lord, please bring Jason home safely. Please help Shane. He's a good man.*

He pulled back, a fragile control in place. "I'm going to get my car keys and check the school."

"Would he know the way?"

"He has a great sense of direction. The other place he might go to is the church."

"I'll go with you. Those places are big. Two of us can cover them faster. What about the police?"

Shane sighed heavily. "I'm also going to call them and grab my cell. The neighbors are going to continue to search around this area. They'll call me if they find him."

Trailing Shane into the house, Whitney wanted to make sure that Louise was okay. She found her in the kitchen at the table, staring at its surface. The older woman looked up, a brief eager hope flashing into her eyes until she saw Whitney's face.

"You didn't find him." Louise dropped her head. "Please, Heavenly Father, take Jason under Your wings and protect him from harm. Please bring him home to us. Amen," she murmured, then repeated the words.

Whitney settled her hand on the woman's shoulder. "We'll find him."

"I should have set the alarm. I should have been in the den. I should…"

Sitting in the chair next to Louise, Whitney clasped the woman's arm, drawing her around toward her. "Listen to me. It isn't your fault. Don't waste time beating yourself up about this. I promise you we'll find him." If she had to scour the whole city, she would come back with the boy.

Determined to fulfill her promise, Whitney put her hands on the tabletop and pushed herself to a standing position. She lifted her gaze to the bay window, the shades still open. The darkness outside taunted her with the added danger to Jason. She skirted the table to draw the blinds. As she reached for the pull cord, something in the backyard caught her attention. Doggie lay half in and half out of his doghouse. Squinting as though that would improve her eyesight, she examined it closer. Something was next to the animal, the dog partially hiding it.

She swirled around. "Did you check the backyard?"

Louise's head shot up. "No. I didn't think about it. I…" She struggled to her feet.

"I'll check it. Does Doggie have a large toy? Possibly a stuffed animal? One Jason gave him?"

"No, not that I know of." Louise stepped to the window and looked out.

Grasping her flashlight, Whitney opened the back door and switched on her light, as well as the porch's.

"Where are you going?" Shane asked, coming into the kitchen.

"To check the backyard. No one has yet."

Shane strode to the door and followed Whitney outside.

"Something in the doghouse caught my attention." She headed straight for it.

Doggie saw them approaching and crawled out. His whole body wiggled as he wagged his tail. Whitney trained her light on the doghouse entrance, illuminating Jason rolling over and rubbing his eyes then looking at them. His pet licked his face, and he giggled.

Shane rushed past Whitney and scooped his son into his arms, his face buried in the crook of Jason's shoulder. "Thank You, Lord. Thank You."

Awed by the power of God, Whitney stood back, giving Shane some privacy while she gathered her own composure. A tear slipped down her cheek. For years, crying had been a wasted release of emotions to her, but since coming to Cimarron City, something inside her had changed. First with her niece and now Jason, she cried. Averting herself, she knuckled the tears away.

Shane carried Jason to her. "Before Doggie came here, Jason never used to come out in the backyard much unless Aunt Louise or I was out here. Next time this will be the first place I look. I plain forgot about it."

"Shane, the police are here," Aunt Louise said from the doorway, a tired smile on her face.

Jason yawned and laid his head on his father's shoulder. That was the best sight Whitney had seen in years. She realized in just a short span of time that she had come to care deeply for the child. Earlier when she had visualized the child hurt, or worse, her heart had constricted with such pain. Just thinking about it again brought a swell of fresh tears to her eyes. She blinked them away and went into the house.

Whitney sat in the church parking lot the next day, staring at the building. She wanted to come personally and offer the Lord thanks and praise for keeping Jason safe. But she couldn't move from her VW. The bells pealed, announcing the service was about to start.

I'm not worthy of going inside. I can't do this. I...

She wasn't like the others. If they knew, they would throw her out of the sanctuary. She started her engine.

And yet the Lord had heard her prayer last night and answered it. Maybe if she sneaked into the back of the church after it began, would God accept her presence in such a holy place?

Tap. Tap.

Gasping, she jerked around to find Shane at her car window, indicating she roll it down.

"You didn't say anything about coming to church today. We could have ridden together." His grin encompassed his whole face. "I have a lot to be thankful for and would love for you to join us."

Jason and Louise flanked him, expectant looks on their faces.

The urge to flee lingered. For months Noah and his family had tried to get her to come to church with them, but she didn't feel she had a right even though she was intrigued by what they had told her about Jesus.

But surely the Lord couldn't forgive people who had really sinned. She could remember being told by her adopted parents only good people went to heaven. With her life she had to have used up her quota of forgiveness.

"Whitney, come." Jason smiled, showing a newly missing front tooth.

"When did you lose your tooth?"

"Got up."

More and more, Jason was talking to her. She'd felt as though he'd given her a gift of words, something most others didn't get.

The bell tolled again.

Shane opened her door. "We'd better get moving. My aunt refuses to be late."

With a deep breath, Whitney slipped from behind her steering wheel and joined them. Inside, the service was starting, so the foyer was empty except for an elderly couple. Good, they would have to sit in the back, and she could leave quickly at the end.

But when they entered, Louise marched right up the center aisle to the second pew where there was barely enough room for them. Whitney's shoulder pressed against Shane's. Worse she glanced sideways and spied Noah and his family all staring at her. Heat scored her cheeks.

She would have some explaining to do afterward.

Shane bowed his head at the end of the service. *Father, thank You for watching over my son. I don't know what I would have done if I'd lost another child. I...* Emotions he could never put into words jammed his throat closed. He peered up at the cross. The sight pierced him with hope.

When the choir finished the last song and filed out of the church sanctuary, people started following. Whitney was the first in their pew to leave, and Shane had to hurry his steps to keep up with her.

"Hey, what's the rush?" he asked, caught in the crowd in the foyer. The sight of her earlier in the parking lot had elated him. The Lord had helped him through a difficult time. He could help heal the pain Shane occasionally glimpsed in Whitney.

"It's over. Time to go."

He looked back at his aunt and son weaving their way through the people at the back of the church. "We usually stay for coffee and snacks. It's a great time to talk to others. Get to know the parishioners. I hope you'll stay."

"I've got a lot to do before I go to the refuge this afternoon." Whitney's gaze lit upon something behind him.

He glanced back again and saw Noah homing in on his sister. "Is there something wrong between you and your brother?"

"Why would you say that?" She sidled toward the double doors that led outside.

"Oh, I don't know. Maybe the way you're acting."

Jason rushed to her side and grabbed her hand, tugging her toward the rec hall. "Eat and drink, Whitney."

He couldn't have planned his son's intervention better. As he trailed after the pair, her brother joined him. "It's good to see you again, Noah. Where are Cara and the kids?"

Noah jerked his thumb in the direction behind him. "Taking up the rear while I'm trying to catch my sister. Cara had something to talk with the reverend about, and the children scattered, meeting up with some of their friends. How did you get her here?"

"I didn't really. I found her in the parking lot before the service and invited her to join us inside. I think she was debating with herself whether to come in or not."

"Good. At least you got her to come in. I've been trying ever since she came to town last November." Noah nodded toward Jason still dragging Whitney toward the table set up with the refreshments. "I see your son has a certain influence over her."

"I think it's hard for her to tell him no."

"I wish I had that touch."

So do I. Whitney was always helping him, but he'd had to fight for every little concession with her. She was afraid to trust. He hoped the Lord taught her how to put trust in Him, then trusting others would come. He'd been down that road and knew where she was coming from.

"I'd better go rescue her before he drags her to his favorite place outside in the garden. With the temperature heading back up into the high nineties, she probably wouldn't appreciate that."

"Not my sister. She doesn't like to sweat."

"Really? Then she doesn't exercise?" He'd been thinking about asking her to go bike riding with him and Jason. If she didn't have a bicycle of her own, she could use his aunt's.

"Swimming is about all I've seen her do. Which she told me was ideal for her."

"The water takes care of the sweat problem," Shane said with a chuckle. "Leave it to her to come up with that solution."

"Tell my sister I'll talk to her later when I don't have to chase her through a crowd."

"Will do." Shane threaded his way toward Jason and Whitney, both filling their plates with food.

Her gaze fell on him then swept the area behind him. Why was she avoiding her brother? He intended to ask her and hoped for once she would confide in him. He'd try to get her alone and have a real conversation with her where there was give-and-take on both sides. It was about time he discovered more about Whitney because his son wanted her in their life.

And maybe he did, too.

Chapter Eight

"That's Bosco, my brother's, Timothy's, cat," Lindsay explained to Jason as Whitney climbed into the tree house, a sprawling tri-level structure, and crawled over to the lowest platform that they sat on.

Shane's son held the small white-brown-and-black cat in his lap, stroking it.

"Hi, Aunt Whitney. Are you through helping Mom with the food?"

"Yeah, I think. It takes a lot to feed a horde of kids."

The little girl giggled. "That's what she's been saying for weeks."

"Jason, I told your dad I would check on you. He's still with Noah, grilling the hamburgers. Everything okay?"

The boy finally swung his attention to Whitney who knelt in front of him. "Bosco soft."

"We're doing fine. I'm helping Jason get to know Bosco." Lindsay straightened her shoulders and sat up tall.

Whitney ruffled her seven-year-old niece's hair. "Thanks for helping Jason."

"He's a friend."

Whitney glanced toward the boy one more time before leaving and saw a new ID bracelet on his wrist, its silver catching the sunlight streaming through the window while Jason petted the cat. "Jason, where did you get this? I like it." She noticed some information about the child was engraved on it.

"Daddy. Can't take it off," he muttered as he ran his hand down the animal, over and over in a rhythmic pattern.

"When's lunch?" Lindsay asked.

"I think your daddy is gonna blow a horn when it's time since everyone is scattered around the estate."

Whitney started to descend the ladder but Andy, Timothy and Rusty were climbing up. She moved back from the opening and allowed the boys onto the first level of the tree house.

"Passing through," Rusty, one of her brother's adopted children, said.

"I wondered where Bosco was hiding." Timothy,

Cara's son from a previous marriage, paused to pet his cat.

"Jason is taking care of him. He's okay." Lindsay slid closer to Jason as though to protect him.

"Great." Timothy hurried after Andy and Rusty.

Whitney finally made her way down the ladder backward and almost fell into Shane's arms when he put his hand on a rung next to her near the bottom. Surprised, she quickly caught herself before both of them ended up on the ground.

"I was coming to see what was taking so long. I thought there might be a problem." He retreated a few steps away.

She hopped off the last rung and faced him. "Jason's fine," she said, her hand over her heart, "but I'm not so sure about me. You surprised me."

"Don't you look before coming down? I thought maybe we were going to maneuver around each other."

"I was hurrying before someone else came up."

"Who's up there with Jason?"

"My niece has decided to take him under her wing. They are together with Bosco."

"I wondered how long it would take him to hunt down the cat after spending most of the morning with Molly."

"Molly is a lovely dog. Your son does have a way of making a beeline to all the animals." She peered toward the area where four grills were set up. "Are you finished cooking?"

"Almost. I need to get back. Lunch is in fifteen minutes."

"Thanks for the heads up," she said as Shane jogged toward his grill.

Whitney surveyed the back lawn at Noah's estate. At least fifty children ran, swam, fished and played games all over the area. The adults had strategically placed themselves so they could monitor the kids' activities. This being her first attendance at Noah's Labor Day shindig, she was amazed everything was running so smoothly, but then Noah and Cara were efficient and organized, not two of her best traits.

She spied Lisa by the pool, sipping a tall glass of lemonade. Whitney checked to make sure her sister-in-law did indeed have everything under control and noted most of the food was on the long tables, ready for consumption by fifty hungry children before Whitney made her way to her friend Lisa.

Whitney sat in the chair across from Lisa in the shade under the large red umbrella. "I haven't had a chance to see how your new job is going. How's being manager working out for you?"

"A lot of hard work, but I'm enjoying the extra challenges." Lisa grinned. "Not to mention the added money a manager makes. This is the first year I've been able to buy Andy the items he's needed for the start of school. He's growing so fast. It's hard to keep him in jeans."

"He mentioned to me he would like to play basketball. With his growth spurt, that might be a good sport for him."

"Yeah, I'm looking into a recreational league that starts in October. I think I can swing the fees if I watch my pennies."

Whitney rested her chin in her palm, her elbow on the table. "It isn't easy being a single mom."

"It isn't easy being a mom period. I've made some big mistakes with Andy. But then I didn't have a good role model. She was never around, and when she was, she was taking drugs. At sixteen, not long after I had Andy, she introduced me to them."

"I didn't have a good role model, either, but mine was because my mother left right after I was born."

"And your dad never remarried?"

Talking to Lisa felt right. "No way. No one would want him. He was a drunk, who liked to get angry when he drank. I was one of his victims." After the words were uttered, surprise fluttered through her. She'd never told another person about what it had been like with her father. Not even she and Noah had discussed it much.

"We're a pair, aren't we? Too bad there wasn't some safe place like Stone's Refuge for us when we were growing up."

Whitney tried not to think about "what ifs" because it didn't make any difference. "I played the hand dealt me." Not necessarily well.

"I know what you mean. I'm still amazed at times that my son loves me. Like the Lord, Andy's love seems to be bountiful."

There was no such thing as love being bountiful. Not in her experience. But then she didn't have a son like Lisa.

Lisa chuckled and leaned closer to her. "Before today I've never used the word *bountiful,* but I'm working on improving the words I use.

"Where I worked in Dallas, I didn't have much of a chance of improving my vocabulary. But since going to college, I've been working on that, too."

The blare of a horn split the noisy air. Although she had expected it, Whitney jumped at the sound. "I guess it's time to eat."

"Your brother has an effective way of getting our attention."

"Leave it to Noah to come up with a bullhorn. I see that Shane is still grilling. I'm gonna check and see if Lindsay and Jason are coming down to eat." Since loud noises could scare Jason, Whitney wanted to make sure he was okay.

"I've seen you and Shane together a lot. In fact, didn't you come with him today? Are you two dating?"

The question took her off guard. "No, we're just friends." And yet, when she declared that to Lisa, she caught Shane looking at her with a warmth in his eyes that made a mockery of her statement.

"I'm stuffed. After that feast, all I want to do is take a nap." Shane stretched his legs out and patted his stomach, watching the crowd milling about the estate, some finished with their lunch, others still eating. "Whoever grilled the hamburgers did a great job."

"One of the best burgers I've had in a long time." Whitney wiped her mouth with her napkin then plopped it on her paper plate. "My compliments to the chef. Louise may have some competition for her job."

"Oh, I think she's safe. Grilling steaks, chicken, ribs and hamburgers is about it for me."

"Louise is certainly enjoying herself today." Whitney gestured across the pool area to a table in the shade.

Shane caught sight of his aunt, sitting with Alice Henderson, the inspiration for Stone's Refuge. A smile graced his aunt's face. "Yeah, she doesn't get out like she should. She devotes so much of her time to us and I can't get her to do anything differently. I really appreciate what she's done for us."

He owed her so much, and when he'd found her on the floor, he glimpsed what it would be like to lose her. He'd lost too many people in his life. It was so much better if he didn't care about others. He needed to remember that when he was around Whitney. His common sense seemed to flee in her presence.

"When I saw Jason earlier, he was wearing an ID bracelet. He told me he couldn't take it off. Good idea about the bracelet. If he runs off, people will know who he is."

Shane remembered the terror he'd felt searching for his son and not finding him. "Before the other night he had identifying information sewed into his clothes. For a long time he wouldn't have worn any kind of bracelet, but in the past six months he has been interested in things like watches. I decided to try this and see if it works. The best thing about the bracelet is that it has a locator device in it. I'll have a means of tracking him if he disappears again."

"That should give you some peace of mind."

"Now I just have to get him in the routine of wearing it at all times. If he gets into the habit, everything should be all right."

"I'll reinforce it with him when I'm working with him." Whitney gathered their trash and rose. "I promised Cara I would help her clean up. What she doesn't know is that I'm gonna get some of the children to help. It shouldn't take too long then."

"That will depend."

He sipped at his iced tea and enjoyed a piece of chocolate pie, his aunt's contribution to the party. The rich dessert melted in his mouth. He sighed and lounged back in his chair, content. Lindsay was dragging his son around and showing him everything. What surprised him was that Jason followed her. Of course, the fact that she usually had some pet in her arms was probably the reason. They both loved animals, which would make Lindsay appealing to his son. At the moment she pulled a gerbil out of a cage and presented Jason with it.

"Get her!" a young boy yelled.

Shane sat up straight and twisted around in time to see Molly running away from Andy, who had been holding her leash, and racing toward the food table where a few hamburgers were stacked on a plate, as well as a cake, several pies and some cookies. Andy dove for the end of the dog's chain but missed. Rusty ran after his pet, but Molly leaped and landed in the middle of the desserts. The table crashed to the ground as the dog lunged for the chocolate pie not far from her mouth.

Shane bolted to his feet. He hurried toward the chaos as Noah snatched the leash and pulled the dog off the collapsed table.

The remnants of food were scattered all over the lawn by the playground. Laughter erupted.

"I wanted to keep Molly in the garage, but Rusty promised me he would keep her under control." Noah swept his arm across his body. "Remind me not to listen to children. Does this look like 'under control' to you?"

Shane fought to contain his own laughter. "No, more like a big mess."

"Yeah, and guess who is gonna clean it up?"

"Rusty."

"Yep." Noah stalked over to his son and shoved the leash into his hand.

Shane peered at the ruined chocolate pie. A weakness but one he certainly enjoyed. At that moment Whitney came into view. Another weakness of his. He watched her move among the children recruiting them to help her clean up. She was a natural with them. She even had Lindsay and Jason stop playing with the gerbil long enough to assist in the clean up. The kids really listened to her and responded to her, especially his son.

Shane stared down at his wedding band. He tried to picture his wife the day she'd slipped it on his finger. For a moment he couldn't remember exactly how she'd looked. Panic rocked his composure. She'd been his one true love. Her light brown hair had been pinned up…no, she'd worn it down because that was the way he'd liked it the best. Yes, slowly an image of Becka at the altar with him materialized, but the fact he'd forgotten in the first place bothered him. What was happening to him? Was it time to let her go? Could he?

"You are definitely a hard lady to get alone. There are always tons of people within earshot," Shane said as he approached her in the gazebo on her brother's estate.

Whitney scanned the area. "I do believe you have me alone now. No one is within thirty yards. Quite a feat for this shindig."

He slid onto the seat near her. "I had you pegged as a loner from the beginning, but for a loner you certainly have a lot of people around you. Even when we ate lunch together, people kept stopping by to chat."

"That happens when you have four nephews and one niece, not to mention all the children and others connected with Stone's Refuge."

"And there's Jason."

"Ah, yes, there's your son."

Shane had decided he wouldn't mince words

with her. He spent all week wrestling with the question of what he wanted concerning Whitney. He wanted her in their lives—his son's, of course, but also his life. For the first time in years he wondered what it would be like if he remarried, if he had a deeper relationship with a woman, beyond friendship. Although he didn't think anyone could replace Becka, maybe the Lord had sent him Whitney to show him there were many facets to love. Because he had no doubt God was behind this extraordinary woman being a part of his life.

"Jason missed you at church yesterday. I missed you. We were hoping you would sit by us again."

She stared down at her lap, clasping her hands. "I had some studying to do before I went to the ranch in the afternoon."

He tried to read her expression, but she'd become good at veiling it. Perhaps a survival technique when she was around so many people all day? Whitney seemed to have a lot of survival techniques in her arsenal to keep her distance from others. Although she was quick to help others, she always kept part of whom she really was locked up inside. And that part was what he was most interested in because it held the key to her trust issues. How was he ever going to show her the importance of putting her trust in the Lord if he didn't know what he was up against?

"What aren't you telling me, Whitney?"

She kept her gaze focused on her white knuckles, unable to put her unworthiness into words. There wasn't enough forgiveness in anyone to ignore her past life and truly accept her. Not even the Lord. And certainly not Shane.

With his forefinger he lifted her chin so she had to look him in the eyes. "What are you struggling with? I can see it in your eyes. I especially noticed it when you were talking with Lisa earlier."

She closed them for a moment, wishing she could regain the blasé facade she'd become so good at presenting to the world—before Cimarron City. If she had known returning to her birthplace would have opened such a wide fissure in the wall around her heart, she would have bypassed the town because the rift brought pain and emotions she'd suppressed for most of her life to the surface. She wasn't equipped to deal with the consequences, but Noah and his family had persuaded her to stay with their acceptance and love.

"Statistics. That course is gonna do me in." She attempted a smile that died on her lips as she peered into Shane's caring gaze.

"I'm quite good in math. I can help you if you want."

She tore her look from his face. "I might take you up on it."

He sighed. "I don't think it's statistics, however, that has you really bothered."

"You aren't gonna let this go, are you?"

"Nope. Last week when you were sitting in your car in the parking lot at church, I watched you for a few minutes. I didn't know whether I should approach you or not. I felt like you were fighting some kind of battle. Does it have to do with the Lord? If so, I might be able to help. I've been there not that long ago."

Can you change what I've done? Can you rewrite my history? She couldn't ask those questions, because she never wanted him to know about her previous life. If she kept him at a distance, she could keep her secrets. But if they grew closer, he would never give up until he knew every sordid bit of her past life.

"What happened to you? I thought you've believed all your life," Whitney said, resorting to a tactic she often used to divert attention from her.

Pain flashed in his eyes. He shifted forward, looking toward the lake. "I suppose I believed. I went to church and went through the motions. My wife, Becka, was very devoted, and I wanted to please her. But all that changed five years ago when Becka died in a house fire caused by an arsonist. She was seven months pregnant with a little girl we both wanted badly. We had even named her Rachel."

His bombshell pierced her as though a piece of shrapnel had punctured her heart. She'd known his wife had died but not how or the fact that at the same time he'd lost a child, too. "I'm so sorry. If you don't want to talk about it, I certainly understand." She wanted to touch him, but his rigid posture forbade her.

"I managed to get Jason out of the house and tried to go back in, but I couldn't. The firefighters held me back. It was burning fast. I was hurt, and they wanted the paramedics to see to me. I begged the Lord to make it go away, to save Becka and our little girl. Afterward, I blamed Him for not doing what I asked. My wife was so passionate about the Lord. Why her and not me? I thought He would save her of all people."

"Why didn't He save her?"

"It was Becka's and Rachel's time to join the Lord. He had other plans for me that didn't include my wife or my daughter."

"And you can accept that?"

"I have to. I can't see His bigger picture. He knows what's best, better than anyone. Certainly better than me. It took me a long time to understand that and to accept it." He glanced toward her. "Actually I might not have if it wasn't for Aunt Louise planting herself in my life. I wanted to hate and rail at everyone. She wouldn't let me. I owe her my spiritual life. Before, I had been so busy trying to please my wife where the Lord was concerned that I forgot it wasn't about that. If I wanted a relationship, it had to be because I wanted it because of what He could do for me and vice versa." One corner of his mouth tilted upward. "That's not to say I didn't put up a hard fight to remain miserable and in pain. But the Lord wouldn't let me go."

"God's never had me." *I'm not good enough for Him.*

"Then what are you struggling with?"

"I felt I owed Him thanks for protecting Jason. I wanted to tell Him so I came to church last Sunday."

"You can thank Him anywhere."

True, and she knew that from Noah. Then why had she gotten up that morning determined to visit the church? "But a church is a house of God."

"The Lord is everywhere. The whole world is His house."

She pushed to her feet and took several steps away. Confusion gripped her—like the past week. She'd even picked up a Bible that Noah had given her and had read several chapters in it, looking for something. She still wasn't sure what she needed or wanted, but her life was in such a turmoil right now that she was seeking answers.

"Maybe if you talk with our minister, he could answer some of your questions."

She whirled around to face him. "No! I won't talk to a stranger, even a minister. I don't bare my soul to anyone."

"Start with the Lord then. Bare your soul to Him. It goes no further than Him."

"Why should He care about me?"

"Because He cares and loves *all* His children."

"What if you're the bad seed, the one thrown away?" She pivoted and hurried from the gazebo, ignoring Shane's call for her to stop.

Tears blurred her vision as she desperately searched for a place to go that didn't have a crowd of people. She sought the back way into the guesthouse, stripped of most of its furniture, and locked the door so she could be alone. Trembling, she collapsed into a lounger in the living room.

At fifteen when she had lived on the streets, she had sold herself for a while in order to eat. It had left her feeling so dirty that she had decided she would rather starve than make some money that way, but the damage had been done. She'd never been able to scrub that dirty feeling from her soul. The memory of that first man touching her produced a well of tears from the depth of her being. They flowed down her cheeks. Any innocence she'd had was gone forever.

How can the Lord forgive that?
I can't even forgive myself.

The sound of the front door being unlocked sent her to her feet. Swiping at the tears that wouldn't stop, she frantically looked around for a place to hide from whoever was coming in. She started to turn and head out the back.

Shane slipped inside.

Trapped, she froze.

His gaze riveted to her. He crossed the distance between them in three, long strides. "Please let me help you. You've done so much for my son and me. I can't stand to see you cry."

Sniffling, she tilted up her chin, brushing the last of her tears from her face. "There, you don't have to."

"Ah, the tough lady is back." He clasped her upper arms. "Crying is good for the soul."

"So you've done it lately?"

"Well, no."

"Then don't lecture me on the value of crying." Having always felt tears were a weakness she couldn't afford, she yanked herself free and hurried toward the door. Escape was all that she could think of before she broke down again and actually told him the awful thing she had done when she'd been desperate. She could never do

that. She never wanted to see his disgust and con-
demnation in his eyes.

He caught her and swung her around. "What did
you mean by 'being a bad seed'? Nothing I've seen
of you is even remotely that. You are kind and
caring. My son, the children at the refuge, wouldn't
love you so much if that weren't the case."

His declaration destroyed the dam she had
quickly erected around her wavering emotions.
The tears returned, a lifetime of them. The ones
she had kept suppressed each time she had taken
money from a man.

He dragged her to him and held her close. She
cried for her lost childhood. She cried for what she
had been forced to do to survive in a world that
had been cruel to a fifteen-year-old. She cried
because she was damaged goods that no man
would ever truly want.

When Shane's shirt was wet and the tears dried
to a few sniffles, she pulled back and stared into
his dear face—a face that occupied her dreams of
what could have been if she wasn't who she was.
She wouldn't allow herself to care—to love—
because she couldn't take the pain of his rejection.

Could she accept the friendship and not want
more?

A pounding at the door drew them both around
to stare at it until Shane walked over and opened

it. Jason flew into the room and threw his arms around Whitney.

"He was worried when he couldn't find you two so I brought him over here," Noah said, then quietly closed the door to give them privacy.

She hugged the child to her. Yes, she would accept the friendship for as long as Shane would offer, and if she longed for something else, she would just have to learn to do without.

"Hey, did you think we left without you, tiger?" Whitney asked, forcing a smile.

Jason nodded. "Can't find."

Shane swung his son up into his arms and around in a circle. "You can't get rid of me, buddy. We're stuck together."

"Like glue?"

Shane set his son down. "Yeah, like glue," he murmured, his gaze fastened on her—like glue.

Chapter Nine

"Shane, you're gonna be sore if you keep bouncing so much in the saddle." Whitney stood in the middle of the ring at Stone's Refuge, observing both father and son as she instructed them. "Watch your son. He's got the hang of it."

"He's been doing it longer."

"Hold the reins looser."

Shane did as she said and one slipped from his grasp.

"Not that loose." She strode to his horse, now in a slow walk, and clasped the rein dangling to the ground. After making sure the two straps were even, she tied them together in a loose knot, what she'd done for Jason at the beginning. "Here try again. This should help you keep the reins together. You shouldn't drop them now. And relax. You're supposed to be enjoying yourself."

A forced grin appeared on his face. "Does this look like I'm enjoying myself?"

"I think your son will be ready for the rodeo. I just don't know about you." She shook her head, hooking her hair behind her ears.

He trotted the horse toward her, pulling *way* back on the reins to halt the horse next to her. Leaning down, he lowered his voice and said, "Jason can't be in the rodeo unless I'm with him."

"Why not? There are other events beside the timed ones."

"Because I..." He narrowed his eyes on her. "Because I said so."

"Quit being so protective. Jason will be all right. You can be near. Maybe in the entrance into the arena." An idea flashed into her mind. "Or you could be a rodeo clown in the arena."

His look evolved into a glare. "Just because I don't have the same kind of ability as my son does with animals doesn't mean I can't learn. I am *not* dressing as a clown. I've seen what they do at a rodeo."

"We could work together on it. I'll teach you some clowning techniques in case the calf in the calf-riding competition bucks his rider off and gets feral. You can save the day." She winked at him, needing to ease the tension emanating from him.

He straightened. "And you aren't going to sweet-talk me into agreeing to your suggestion."

"Okay, then you'd better be prepared to work hard or you'll be eating your son's dust."

"I'd planned on racing behind him anyway."

"How about way behind him in the goat-tying competition?"

Shane blinked rapidly. "Goat tying? We haven't practiced that yet."

"All in good time."

"Whitney, look." Jason maneuvered Big Red around the barrel at one end of the large paddock.

"That's wonderful! I think your dad has had enough riding today. Let's call it quits. We'll practice again tomorrow before we go on our Sunday ride. Okay?"

Jason nodded and guided his gelding toward the gate.

She loped over to it and opened it. "Cool him off and put him in his stall."

Shane headed toward her as Jason rode to the large maple to cool down his horse.

Shutting the gate, she faced Shane. "You can ride around the ring again and try to increase your speed past a slow walk."

"I thought you said I'd had enough of riding."

"I did and you have, but one more time before

you stop. That, or I'll show you how to put on clown makeup."

"But shouldn't someone watch Jason?"

"Peter is in the pen with a new goat. He'll take care of Jason if he needs it."

"But—"

"Clown or practice." She jammed her hands onto her waist and glared at him.

"Okay, but just one time. I have a feeling I'm going to be sore tomorrow."

"I can guarantee you will be."

Frowning, he nudged the gait of his gelding up to a trot. She almost laughed out loud at his grimace that occurred each time his bottom slapped the saddle. The sound echoed through the yard.

When he reached one end of the paddock, Whitney called out, "Go all the way around the barrel as close as you can." She wasn't sure if he would be the rider or Jason in the barrel pickup, so she needed both of them to practice going around the metal container.

His path was at least six feet from the barrel, and instead of going in a full circle, his horse shot forward halfway around and headed for the gate.

"Whoa," Shane said, and yanked back on the reins.

The animal kept going, increasing his speed.

"Show him who is in control," she shouted, and ran toward the pair.

"He is," Shane called back over his shoulder.

One final time he pulled on the reins. The gelding came to such an abrupt halt that Shane nearly went over its head into the fence. He clung to the horse's neck, then it dropped its head and dragged him down, the reins all but forgotten in his desperation to keep himself from falling. But his weight was too far forward, and he tumbled to the ground. Dust billowed up from his hard impact. He coughed and lay there while the gelding nudged at the gate nearby.

Whitney hurried to Shane. "Are you all right?"

He waved his hand in front of his face as the dust cloud settled on him. "Can we call it quits now?"

Pressing her lips together to contain her laughter at the pitiful look he gave her, she offered him her hand. "We'll try again tomorrow at one o'clock."

He groaned and placed his hand in hers.

She yanked him to a standing position, then grabbed the horse's reins before opening the gate.

Shane slapped the dust from his shirt and jeans while trailing her from the paddock.

When she approached the maple tree, she glanced back at Shane to make sure he truly was okay. He wasn't limping which was a good sign. "Jason, you can put Big Red into his stall. Ask Peter to show you the new goat." The child hadn't learned yet when to stop walking his horse. If she hadn't said anything he would have continued on and on.

As she began cooling down Shane's horse, she heard him say to Jason, "Don't walk so close to Big Red."

Shane then made his way toward the maple. With his attention on his son going into the barn, he nearly ran into the tree.

"Shane, watch where you're going," she shouted on the other side of the maple.

He swung his gaze around and halted a few feet from the trunk.

"Jason is safer here than you are. Not much experience with animals or ranches?"

"None with ranch life and little with animals. My father was allergic to cats and dogs. I did have a snake once until it got loose in the house. My mom had a fit. How about you? You're good with them. You must have grown up with lots of pets."

Her father would have used an animal against her. "Hardly. I didn't even have a snake." Bitterness crept into her voice that she quickly tried to mask by saying, "But I'm changing that. Once Calico gets used to the apartment, I'm getting another kitten from here. There are certainly plenty to choose from. Peter seems to always have a litter dumped at his ranch. How about you? Another dog?"

His eyes widened. "I don't think so, at least not for a while. Jason's great with Doggie, but I don't want to overwhelm him."

"Are you sure you're talking about your son?"

He chuckled. "I like a routine, too. Animals seem to throw them off."

"Unpredictable?"

"Sometimes. Just the other day Doggie darted out the gate before I had a chance to grab him. He'd never done that, and I ended up chasing him up and down the street. I'm surprised you didn't see me."

"I'm sorry I missed it," she said, laughter tingeing her voice. "Or better yet, I wish I had a video camera to record the event."

"Humph. Go right ahead and have a good laugh on me. I can take it."

She ambled to him, thrust the reins into his hands then sauntered toward the barn. "You are fun to tease, especially when it comes to animals."

"Hey, I can't help it if I'm clueless about them." He hurried after her with his gelding trailing behind him.

"Starfire belongs in there." Whitney gestured toward the second stall but kept walking.

"What do I do? Just stick him inside?"

She turned and backpedaled. "Don't forget to shut the gate quickly. If you don't, he's just like

Doggie, and I'd hate to see you chasing a horse around the yard."

The look of horror that descended on Shane's face made her laugh even more. She swung around and went in search of Jason and Peter. Just as she suspected, they were with the new goat in the fenced field at the side of the barn. The new goat's front half was black and its back half was white. Not far from the gate, Jason rubbed his face against the kid that had been born a few weeks ago at the ranch.

"The new goat's cute. The children will enjoy her. They gravitate toward the smaller ones." Whitney entered the large pen Peter had constructed for his goats and sheep. "Is she full grown?"

"Yeah, this breed runs smaller than others."

"What kind—"

"I barely got out of the stall. Starfire charged toward the door. I haven't moved that fast in ages." Shane entered the pen with a small dog on his heels. He tried to close the gate before the mutt got inside.

But the animal Whitney hadn't seen around the ranch surged forward, barking at the goats and sheep. They scattered. The new one fell over, rolled and landed on its side, her stiff legs sticking out.

"Oh, no!" Whitney ran toward the animal while Peter tried to corral the stray.

Shane was right behind her. "What happened?"

"Sleeping like Auntie." Jason continued to hold the kid, beaming with a smile.

Peter grabbed the mixed breed that had caused the ruckus. "The goat's all right."

Just as he said those words, the small animal jumped up and raced toward the others.

"The goat's good," Jason said, stroking the white kid.

A few minutes later Peter returned to the pen. "Sorry about that. I wasn't sure he was a fainting goat. I've never had one. Just heard about them."

"I guess now you know, but what's a fainting goat?" Whitney stood next to Shane, her expression probably as perplexed as his.

"This particular breed when startled will involuntarily stiffen for maybe ten seconds or so. Some will fall over like that one did. Some, I've heard, have learned to compensate for the genetic quirk."

"The children will like that."

"Yeah, too much." Peter pushed his hand through his hair. "Which gives me a dilemma. With all that goes on here, I'm afraid the goat will spend a lot of time on the ground."

"Maybe she'll be one that compensates." Whitney found the animal under discussion now grazing on a patch of grass among the sheep.

"Maybe. At the very least I'll have to set up some rules concerning our new addition."

"What about the dog? I haven't seen him around," Whitney said.

"It's a her, and that's the first time I've seen her, which means I have another animal."

"Maybe you can find a home for her. She's cute and could make a nice companion to another dog." Whitney slid a glance toward Shane.

"Don't say that where Jason can hear. I think we'd better be heading home. I can feel my muscles getting stiff and sore as we speak."

She stepped close. "All it's gonna take is Jason to really see the new dog to want it."

"You take her. You're the one who brought Jason out here in the first place."

"Dogs and cats don't mix."

"Sure they do," Peter said, grinning from ear to ear. "They do out here."

Whitney sent her friend a glare. "I'm a cat person."

"Well, in that case, I have several kittens you can pick from in a couple of weeks when they are weaned," Peter added.

"Yeah, she told me she was looking for another one." Shane strode toward his son. "Ready to leave? We still need to go to the grocery store before going home."

Jason placed the kid on the ground next to its mother, then took his father's hand. Shane's son paused next to Whitney. "Church with me."

Although the sentence wasn't worded as a question, Whitney knew that the child wanted her to attend the service with him tomorrow, and she didn't know if she should. He would expect it each week. She hated to disappoint him, and yet she didn't think she would really be accepted if the people knew the truth about her. "I have some stu…" She stared into the boy's upturned face and couldn't say no. "Yes, I'll come."

Jason tugged on her arm until she bent toward him. Then he planted a kiss on her cheek before strolling away.

At the gate Shane peered back at her. "You can ride to church with us."

She nodded, incapable of speech at the moment. For some reason accepting had felt right.

Peter stepped to her side. "I'm glad that Shane brings Jason out here. I'd been trying to get him to for the past year. All he needed was a catalyst. You."

Desperate to change the subject, she checked her watch. "I'm gonna be late for the meeting about the rodeo fund-raiser if I don't get a move on. See you tomorrow." Before Peter said anything about Shane, she rushed from the pen and toward Hannah's house.

She'd forgotten exactly when the meeting was, but she thought it was at four o'clock. Arriving on Hannah's porch, she knocked then turned and noticed that there were no cars in the drive in front of the house. Maybe she'd totally missed it. If so, she'd like to lay the fault at Shane's feet. But she couldn't. She forgot to look that morning at her schedule—something she'd learned to do in order not to be late.

Hannah swung the door open. "You're half an hour early. Come on in and talk to me while I finish baking the cookies."

"Baking cookies for the meeting?"

"I have some for you all but most of them are for the social hour after the service tomorrow. It's my turn to bring some food items."

Whitney took a deep breath of the delicious smell. "Chocolate chip?"

"Yes. My family's favorite. I've got some for them, too, or I'd never hear the end of it." When entering the kitchen, Hannah, the refuge's manager and good friend, crossed to the counter by the stove. "Want anything to drink? If so, help yourself. I have some out for the meeting."

"Do you want me to fix you anything?" Whitney grasped the pitcher of lemonade and poured some into a tall glass. "I'm parched after being at the barn and working with Shane and Jason on riding."

"How's it coming along?"

"I don't know if Shane will be ready in a few weeks for the rodeo. For a man who is capable in most of the things I've seen him do, he's certainly inept at riding a horse."

"Peter said that Jason is doing great."

"Yeah, he didn't get his riding genes from his father. Must have been his mother."

Hannah finished spooning some cookie dough onto a baking sheet, then took one sheet out of the oven while replacing it with the other. "What's going on between you and Shane? I know you've told me you two are friends, but it doesn't look that way to me."

Whitney was in the process of swallowing her drink when Hannah asked that question. She nearly choked and ended up coughing. "We are friends, Hannah. That's all. Haven't you noticed he still wears his wedding ring? Does that sound like a man who wants to be more than friends?"

"I've always seen Shane as a man resistant to change. But he's also a smart man and will figure out you would be good for him."

This time Whitney spewed lemonade all over the kitchen table. "Warn me before you make ridiculous comments like that last one." Snatching the dishcloth from the sink, she mopped up her mess, trying to hide the flushed cheeks from her friend's sharp perusal. Then she sat at the table.

Hannah turned with spatula in hand. "If you're really truthful with yourself, you can't deny the attraction you feel for Shane. Can you?"

Her friend's gaze zeroed in on Whitney, gauging her expression. She wanted to squirm under that scrutiny. "Okay. Okay. He's an attractive man. Satisfied?"

"Nope. All you admitted was how he looked to you. Not how you feel about him."

Restless, Whitney shot to her feet. "I can't get involved with him. Our lives don't gel."

"It looks like they gel to me. For the past month you all have been together a lot. Let me stress that again. *A lot.*"

Whitney didn't know what else to say to Hannah. "He's got a child," she blurted out, not sure where that came from. "And he's still in love with his deceased wife."

"Okay, we're getting some place. I thought you cared about Jason. Does it bother you that he's autistic?"

Does it? Whitney thought back over the past month, dealing with Jason in the classroom, at his house, here at the ranch. "No. You should see that child's potential. In class he's smart. He's way ahead of the others as far as numbers go."

"Then it bothers you about Shane's deceased wife?"

"Look, Hannah, love doesn't exist for people like me." She pivoted to leave and get some fresh air before everyone else showed up for the meeting.

"What kind of people are you referring to?" Hannah's words halted Whitney's flight.

"Ones who don't deserve to be loved." This time Whitney didn't stop until she was outside on the porch, leaning into the railing, inhaling deep, composing breaths. Fighting desperately to keep the tears buried.

"Amanda, I'm so glad you've finally decided to come have coffee with me." Whitney took a chair at a café several blocks from school in the opposite direction of Amanda's place. She'd noticed the few times she'd driven the young woman home that Amanda got tenser the closer they came to where she lived.

Amanda took the seat against the wall, facing out so she could see the people entering the restaurant. "My boyfriend, Hayden, has to work late tonight, so I have some time before I need to get home."

"And you're probably sick of me asking you so you decided to come to shut me up."

The young woman with straight red hair that hung to the middle of her back giggled, her ever-present tension siphoning from her. "No, I've been wanting to come. Just had—things I had to do after school. I've been interested in asking you about going to college. I want to be a teacher, too."

After giving the waitress their orders, Whitney rested her chin in her cupped palm, her elbow on the table. "What questions do you have?"

"One of my biggest concerns is the cost. I've saved very little."

"There are some need-based scholarships I think you would have a good chance of getting. Also there are student loans. The university has a great Financial Aid Office. Call and make an appointment to see them. I'd go with you. That is if your boyfriend doesn't want to."

Her cheeks pale, Amanda tensed. "It was just a dream. It'll be years before it can become a reality."

Whitney waited until after the waitress placed their coffees in front of them to say, "Is your boyfriend abusing you?"

What color was still in Amanda's face leached completely out. She dropped her gaze, her hair falling forward to hide her almost completely from Whitney.

"The reason I ask is because I've been there. I know the signs." Whitney fortified herself with deep breaths. She'd never talked about this to anyone, but Amanda was worth the pain of telling her story. "Amanda, you aren't alone. There are other women who have been abused and finally sought help. I want to help you do that."

"But it's me. It's not Hayden's fault I can't do anything right. Once I get better, he'll be okay."

"I thought that once. It never happens. I was in a really low place in my life and began dating a man who was exactly like my father. He used me for a punching bag until he put me in the hospital one too many times. When you sink to the bottom, thankfully there's only one place to go, up. A woman helped me to come up with a plan to get out. I packed a few items of clothing he wouldn't know were missing and stashed away as much money as I could. One day he was beating on me but thankfully got tired before finishing the job. He left to go see some buddies." The memory stole her breath for a few seconds. She swallowed hard and forced herself to tell Amanda the rest. "I arranged with my benefactor who had my bag with my stash to pick me up if I called and gave her our agreed-upon signal. The day I made that call was the first day of my new life."

Amanda finally made eye contact with her. "Where did you go?"

"To a shelter, and the lady who ran it helped me get a protective order against my boyfriend and eventually assisted me in getting out of town. There are places like that here. They will keep your location a secret and help you set up a new life. I'll help you."

"I don't know, Whitney. All I have to do is keep the house a little neater, make dinners on time…" Her voice faded as her eyes widened.

"You aren't alone." Whitney suddenly remembered Shane saying that to her when he'd offered to help her. Was it possible she'd been so busy trying to be this independent woman that she'd gone too far the other extreme?

The scent of hay, dirt and sweat saturated the air in the rodeo arena. A neighing horse in the stall nearby vied with the roar of the audience in the stands.

Whitney plopped the cowboy hat on Jason's head. "There you go, partner. Are you ready to beat the others?"

The child's attention snagged on the huge steer across the yard, pawing at the ground in his pen. His long horns jutted upward a foot, menacing in an animal. Thankfully the beast was only at the rodeo for exhibition purposes.

"Jason—" Whitney put her hand on his shoulder and waited until he returned his wide gaze to her "—you are not to go near the bull. Besides, we're on after they finish the bull riding. In the goat tying, I'll be right behind you."

The children competed in four events sprinkled among the professional competition. Jason and she would ride in the barrel pickup and goat tying while the older children participated in the calf riding and barrel racing. Shane had volunteered to be one of the clowns in spite of his protests a few weeks ago.

Peter brought Big Red out for Jason to ride in the "competition" while Whitney retrieved Princess Leia from her stall. After climbing on the mounting block, Jason swung into the saddle like a pro. The child had said little since arriving at the arena, but behind his silence he studied everything going on, especially the animals utilized in a rodeo.

As she mounted her own horse, Shane appeared in a black cowboy hat, thick white makeup with large red circles around his eyes and mouth and black tears down his cheeks. But what really caught her attention was his orange shirt with bright lime-green pants. "My, you got creative."

"I'm sure glad I'm not the only one doing this." Shane jerked his thumb toward her brother who had emerged from the trailer where the clowns got ready. "I'm equally glad the children aren't doing any bull riding because I don't know how real rodeo clowns do their job, throwing themselves between bull and rider."

"If there was a bull in the ring, believe me, he would see you coming a mile away."

"At least my job tonight is much easier. However, I objected to being labeled the bad guy. I should have spoken up faster." Shane tipped his black hat then checked his toy gun, twice as big as a normal one, strapped to his thigh. "But I've been practicing. I'm going to be quicker on the draw."

The man who was in charge of the rodeo had felt better if there were a couple of people who were familiar with the kids at the refuge out in the arena when the children ran through their events. Noah said he would and then volunteered Shane who had quickly agreed. Later he discovered this was the clown role Whitney had mentioned.

"You shouldn't have given up on learning to ride a horse. Then you could be doing what I'm going to do."

"That's okay. Riding a horse while it's walking is vastly different from riding any faster. My body was sore for days after that first lesson."

"Chicken. You just wanted to get out of the lessons."

"You're one hard taskmaster. I know when to cut my losses." He looked over at his son. "Goat tying should be a piece of cake. Even I could have done that."

"I think you could have managed getting on and off the horse in a dignified manner, too, if you'd worked at it." Whitney clamped her lips together to keep from breaking out in laughter. She loved to tease Shane. "Let's face it. You have *city slicker* written all over you."

He took his suspenders and stretched them out. "Yep. And proud of it." But when the straps snapped back into place, his eyes grew round and he yelped. "That hurt."

Peter approached. "Time to go, Whitney."

The goat-tying competition went off without any problems. Jason rode his horse to the right place, jumped off and held the goat while she tied its legs. However, when the crowd cheered so loud the sound was deafening, Jason covered his ears and pressed close to Whitney.

When the child was back in the staging area, he acted as though nothing bothered him. "I've noticed at school that he's sensitive to loud noises," Whitney said to Shane when he approached them.

"Mostly any that last over a few seconds can really bother him. Like a siren on an ambulance. I didn't realize how wild the crowd would go for the children."

"Should we do the barrel pickup then?"

"He should be okay. They cheer at the end and by that time he's riding his horse out of the ring. Besides, you'll be behind him on the horse in case there's a problem."

"Are you sure?"

Shane glanced toward his son still sitting on his horse, leaning over and patting its neck. "Yeah. If I told him now he couldn't do it, I *know* he would create a scene. He's been planning on this for weeks."

When the fire alarm at school had gone off for the monthly practice, she'd warned Jason and he had seemed fine. But when it actually sounded, he screamed, held his ears and hid under a table, curled up in a tight ball. She'd thought at the time, it was the high pitch of the sound or the suddenness of it that affected him. She had read about autism, but she'd felt there wasn't one set of characteristics. There were a lot of variables when dealing with a child with autism.

"I shouldn't have gotten him involved if it's gonna cause him anguish, Shane."

"The lessons and everything he's done to prepare for this have made my son happy. I'm glad you persuaded me to let him ride in the rodeo even if you kicked me off the team."

"After your second lesson," she said with a chuckle, "I knew you were a hopeless case, at least in time for the rodeo. Maybe in a year or so you'll figure out how to ride properly."

"Remember, *city slicker* here and proud of it." Shane tapped his chest and smiled.

Half an hour later Peter came to get them for the barrel pickup. Normally she would ride to the barrel and the child would jump on the horse, then she would race back to the finish line. But she'd decided it would be safer for Jason if she waited for him to retrieve her from the barrel, especially since he loved to ride so much.

Whitney jogged into the arena. Shane, dressed as a clown, gave her a leg up onto the barrel then backed off for the race to begin. Jason charged into the ring, Big Red picking up speed as they headed toward her. Approaching her, Jason fastened his gaze onto the yellow barrel beneath her.

Yellow! She'd forgotten about his fascination with the color. She tensed.

As planned, Jason guided his horse straight toward her. Then suddenly, still fifteen feet away, he reached with his hand as though he wanted to touch the yellow barrel. Ten feet away, Jason dropped the reins and leaned sideways toward her, his arm still up. She was supposed to jump onto the horse, not Jason onto the barrel!

Big Red swerved at the last moment, his shoulder bumping into the barrel as he moved aside. The thump rocked the metal container and threw Whitney off balance. As if in slow motion, the barrel teetered. Fear surged through Whitney that she would fall into Jason and maybe break his outstretched arm or knock him off the shying horse. To avoid that, she aimed for a spot clear of the horse and barrel, but the metal container tilted out from under her and foiled her chance for a safe dismount.

The hard contact with the barrel sent a wave of pain through her as she was hurled to the ground. Big Red's back hoof clipped her thigh while he spun around to head toward the finish line. The air rushed from her lungs as the dust kicked up choked her.

Chapter Ten

The second Whitney lost her balance as the barrel pitched back, Shane rushed forward, knowing he couldn't prevent it or catch her. She slammed into the ground, the horse nearly trampling her. His heart thudded in his chest as his breath bottled in his lungs.

Jason's horse shot off to the side while his son hung on to the saddle horn. Peter stopped the horse from trotting down the edge of the ring toward the exit and took charge of them. Satisfied his child was in good hands, Shane turned his full attention to Whitney.

She hadn't moved.

Please, Lord, let her be all right.

He skidded to a halt next to her and knelt. "Whitney?"

Her eyelids fluttered open. She moaned, then

began to cough as the dust and dirt rained down on her.

"Are you okay?"

Nodding, she propped herself up on her elbows. "Just had the wind knocked out of me."

Whitney scanned the growing crowd surrounding her, hating being the center of attention. "I'm fine." She waved the people away. "Where's Jason? Is he okay?"

"He's fine. He's with Peter. Nothing's broken? How about where the horse got you?" Noah asked over Shane's shoulder.

When Whitney moved her legs, then sat completely up and wiggled her arms, she noticed no one had moved away earlier. "Nothing's broken here. You all can go back to your jobs. I'm getting claustrophobic."

When the crowd ambled away, Whitney drew in a deep breath.

"Are you sure nothing's wrong?" Shane stood and offered his hand.

She clasped it and let him pull her up. "My left leg hurts like crazy. I'm gonna have a big bruise where Big Red got me, but I'll be all right. I've had worse injuries."

When she said the last sentence, a shadow flitted in her eyes. She quickly veiled them from him. "You have?" he asked as he assisted her to the exit.

He knew he shouldn't probe, but he really didn't know much about her past. She was such a contradictory woman. One moment tough, the next gentle and kind, willing to help anyone in need.

"There's Jason. I'm so glad he didn't fall off the horse." She limped toward his son.

And again she ignored one of his questions about her past.

What was he wanting from Whitney—really wanting? When he saw her take a hard tumble to the ground, all that ran through his mind was: *I can't lose another person I care about.*

Was that it? Did he want more from their relationship than friendship? He'd been wrestling with that question for weeks. For once he needed to focus on it—away from her beguiling presence—until he had an answer.

"I went fast!" Jason said to Whitney when she reached him.

She ruffled his hair. "That you did. You need to see to Big Red. That was his last competition." She gestured toward Peter who held the gelding's reins. "Remember a rider always sees to his horse's needs."

Jason spun around and raced to Big Red.

Shane watched his son for a few seconds. Jason threw his arms around the small horse's neck and kissed him. "Thank you, Whitney, for getting Jason involved with the animals at the refuge."

"You're welcome. It's so much fun seeing him grow and interact not only with the animals but the other children. He's coming out of his shell more and more. He likes spending time with Lindsay and Andy."

Shane suddenly knew what he should do. "You've been good for my son and in appreciation I want to take you to dinner. Next Saturday night?"

"Dinner? Saturday night? I—I…"

"It's just a thank-you dinner. We talked about going out to dinner when things settled down a while back. Things have settled down. Aunt Louise is back in full force. Jason is settled in school," he said, interjecting as much casualness as he could into his voice. If she thought it was anything but that, she would probably decline the invitation.

"But you want to go out *Saturday* night?"

"And?"

"That's…" She averted her gaze, staring at his son and Peter. Then with a deep sigh, she looked right at him. "That's usually considered a date night."

"But we aren't dating, are we? I'm taking you to dinner. Nothing more, nothing less. People do that without dating."

"Oh." Her eyebrows crunched together as if she were in deep thought. "Okay."

He'd wouldn't have been surprised if she had said no. Only disappointed. But in the next week he needed to come up with a plan. The friendship thing wasn't exactly working. He wasn't sure he was ready for more, and he certainly wasn't sure she was. But he was also tired of skirting every issue of her past. Even if they remained friends only, he wanted more than what she was giving him.

Through the reflection in the dresser's mirror in his bedroom, Shane peered at the alarm clock on his bedside table. He needed to pick Whitney up for their non-date in twenty minutes.

He adjusted his red tie, buttoned his charcoal coat then unbuttoned it. He hadn't worn a suit in months, but he'd told her to dress up, that he was taking her to a nice restaurant. Usually when working with children and young adults, he wore casual clothes, which seemed to put them more at ease during their sessions.

He also hadn't been out to dinner alone with a woman in years. Not since Becka. Panic flooded him at the prospect of the evening ahead. Was it like riding a bike? Would "how to date" all come back to him when he went to pick up Whitney?

"I know. I said it wasn't a date," he said to his image in the mirror. "But this sure feels like one to me."

After picking up a brush, he ran it through his hair. The gold of his wedding band gleamed in the overhead light and caught his attention. He stared at it, his fingers on his left hand splayed. Twirling the ring around and around, he toyed with removing it. He'd never thought he would take it off. He'd made a promise to love and honor his wife. He hadn't counted on her dying, at least not before they had been married for fifty years.

"You need to move on," Aunt Louise said just inside the doorway.

Shane glanced sideways. "I didn't hear you come in."

"No, because you were so deep in thought. Becka would have wanted you to start dating again. To get a life."

He faced her. "I've got a life. I have you, Jason, my practice and my friends."

"You're trying very hard to convince me. Or are you really trying to convince yourself?"

He shifted away. "How can I really move on when I let Becka down?"

"How? Because you lived and she didn't? That wasn't letting her down. Are you questioning the Lord?"

Why did I live when my wife and unborn child didn't? "It shouldn't have happened at all." Guilt blanketed him. He touched his chest, a few visible scars from the fire there as a constant reminder of what happened.

"I was happy that you asked Whitney out. I thought finally you were going to return to the living. Whitney deserves all of you. She's a loving woman who's been great for Jason. I see her love for your son growing every day. If you're not serious, back away from her."

"What about Jason?"

"I'll take care of that. She can still be involved with him." Turning to leave, she paused. "So think long and hard tonight because Whitney doesn't need to be hurt again."

"Hurt again? What do you mean?" Did his aunt know something about her past that he didn't? The thought brought hurt to the foreground. He wanted Whitney to confide in him.

"That girl is carrying around a lot of pain. She's pretty good at hiding it, but remember I volunteered at a shelter for abused women for years, and she has been abused by someone in her past."

Whitney? A protective need expanded through him at the thought that someone might have physically hurt her. His hands curled at his sides.

How had he missed that? He'd sensed her vulnerability and even her pain, but he'd never thought of it as coming from an abusive situation because she was so tough, her need to be independent so strong. Was he too close to her to see really what was going on with her?

His aunt left. The silence mocked him with his declarations that he had a life. Rubbing his hand across his upper chest, the ridges of the scars caused by a burning board beneath his touch, he knew he had to come to a decision once and for all concerning Whitney. He never did things half-heartedly, and Aunt Louise was right. If he dated her past this evening, it would be because he hoped to have a future with her.

I'll make the first move. He tugged on his wedding ring, slipping it from his finger and stashing it in the top drawer in his dresser. Now there were no barriers between them, but what was in their past.

In the end if she couldn't trust him enough with her past, with what was bothering her, it didn't make any difference what he wanted or did. He'd had a marriage where he and his wife had shared everything. He would never settle for less.

After snatching his keys from the dresser, he hurried toward the front door. All this debating with himself was making him late. Not a good way to start the evening.

Whitney had donned one of the few dressy outfits she owned. Its simple lines flared at the waist and the black dress fell in soft folds about the calves of her legs. The three-inch high heels were probably a mistake since she usually only wore flats. Hopefully she wouldn't have to walk much.

The sound of footsteps coming up her stairs filtered to her.

He's here! Her heartbeat increased.

"Well, Calico, what do you think?" She pirouetted in the middle of the living area with her arms spread wide.

Her cat looked at her for a second then went back to grooming herself.

"I'm not sure I like that comment," she muttered, making her way to the door as a knock resonated through the quiet.

She greeted Shane with a smile although the corners of her mouth quivered slightly. She didn't like being so nervous. It wasn't as if she didn't know this man standing in front of her, looking attractive, dignified in a dark gray suit. What surprised her was the bold red tie. Bold color in a subtle statement of gray.

"Ready? I have reservations at seven."

"Let me get my shawl or rather Cara's. I borrowed it." She grabbed the black cashmere wrap and started to don it.

Shane stopped her, took the shawl and draped it over her shoulders. "You look beautiful."

"You're not so bad yourself." She peered back at him and realized her mistake. He was so close, the minty scent of his toothpaste hovered between them. Quickly she moved away, but not before her heartbeat sped even faster.

He cocked a grin. "I'm beautiful?"

She chuckled. "Okay, to appease your male ego, not beautiful but handsome."

"Thank you. I feel so much better." On the stoop Shane allowed Whitney to go down the stairs first.

When she strolled toward his SUV parked at the end of the driveway, his hand rested at the small of her back. His touch zipped through her like the zap of an electric volt. She'd thought about hurrying her pace, but long ago she'd overcome most of her fears and had learned to show none of her misgivings. This "non-date" felt more like a date than any she had ever been on in the past.

Settled in the passenger's seat, she watched him round the front of his car and climb in. "Where are we going?"

"A surprise."

Curious, she thought of several "nice" restaurants, but when he pulled into a quaint inn on the lake outside of town, she was surprised. "Breckinridge Inn is more than nice. It's definitely upscale." Now she was glad she'd purchased the shoes. Her black flats wouldn't have worked.

"I've heard good things about this place. I wanted to try it, and you've given me a reason to." He slipped from behind the steering wheel.

Not used to men opening doors for her, she started to exit the vehicle when he appeared at her side. He quickly assisted her from the car. His hand lingered at her elbow as they made their way to the entrance.

Inside her gaze swept the main room with several alcoves off of it. The dim, artificial lighting was accented with white candles on pedestals of crystal on all the tables. Their flames danced in the shadows, heightening the sense of elegant amenity.

When she was seated at a small table in one of the alcoves, the fine ivory-colored china with gold edging, the goblets with a swirled design etched into them and the gold flatware gave her a surreal feeling as though she were viewing someone else going through the motions of having dinner. The tuxedo-clad waiter took her linen napkin and spread it over her lap, then handed her a menu with no prices on it.

She leaned close to Shane when the older man left. "I feel like a traitor to my brother. Shouldn't we be at one of his restaurants?" *Where I know the prices of every item.*

"I won't tell. Besides, he suggested this place."

She nearly dropped the menu. "He did? When did you see him?"

"At church last week when you were talking with Hannah and Cara after the service."

"Oh, good. I'd hate to cause a rift in my small family."

"Tell me about your family. I don't know much from Noah."

"There isn't much to tell. Noah and his family are all the family I have." She looked behind her. Could she escape before he delved any deeper into her life? She should have seen this invitation for what it was: a time to lure her into a sense of compliancy then, wham, the questions would start.

"I think I remember him telling me you moved here from Dallas. What did you do there?"

Resisting the urge to squirm in her chair, she met his gaze. "I was a bartender, at least at my last job. After getting my GED, I went to college during the day and tended bar at night. The pay was good, which helped me fund my schooling." A defensive edge entered her voice that she wished she could squash.

"Then you probably heard countless stories of people's woes."

"My fair share. Personally I don't know how you do it. I listened, but I couldn't even begin to tell anyone what they should do." *Especially with the mess I made of my life.*

"Listening is half the job. Sometimes people just need someone to hear them."

"And the other times?"

"They need guidance. I don't usually tell them what to do. They have to want to do it or it won't work."

"Have you ever counseled adults?"

He looked away, masking his expression from her. "Once. A lifetime ago. But five years ago, I went back to school and changed my focus to children."

"Why?" she asked, aware the answer would be wrapped up in his wife and her death. The coincidence of her dying five years ago and him changing his focus was too much to ignore.

When he reestablished eye contact with her, his eyes darkened with pain. "Because I felt I could no longer help adults. And before you ask why, I know what you're doing. You're changing the topic of conversation to me." He picked up his ice water and took a drink.

Whitney's gaze fastened onto his left hand and his ring finger, minus his wedding band. The sight stunned her and momentarily stole her intended words. "You aren't wearing your wedding ring," she murmured, instantly wanting to snatch the sentence back.

He spread his fingers wide and peered at his hand.

"No, I guess I'm not." One corner of his mouth tilted in an amused look. "You're quite observant."

"What happened? Why did you take it off?" Panic replaced her defensive tone, her heart pounding in her chest. So long as he'd had it on, she'd been safe from falling in love with him. Now the rules were changed.

The waiter appeared at the table to take their order, forcing Whitney to wait for Shane's answer.

An eternity later when the man left with their selections, Shane took another sip of his water, then said, "This wasn't quite the way I'd planned to go about this, but as I've learned with Jason, I sometimes have to go with the flow. I can't ignore the attraction I feel toward you any longer. I'd like to see where it leads us." He stared at his left hand. "This wasn't a rash decision. Frankly I hadn't planned on removing my wedding ring ever." When he peered deep into her eyes, he added, "I can't date you and wear it."

"What does that mean?"

"I was happily married to Becka. For five years I've been content with the knowledge I had my one true love and that's all there was for me. Now I realize I want more. You made me realize there could be more." He paused.

Still grappling for words, Whitney remained silent, her mind blank.

"Say something."

"This wasn't supposed to be a date!"

"Why does dating really scare you?"

"Because I don't want to get serious. Because..." *With you I could get serious fast.* She couldn't say that! Sighing, she looked around for the waiter. She needed a distraction, an interruption, anything not to have this conversation with Shane. She didn't want to hurt him. She cared about him, too— She collapsed back, stunned at her train of thought.

He watched her but didn't respond to her.

"The main reason I was a bartender was to remind me every day what drinking can do to a person. My father was a mean drunk who loved to take his frustration out on me. I didn't think things could get any worse until the day he just up and left Noah and me. We went into the foster-care system and were separated. I was adopted by a family. Noah wasn't. They moved me away from the only home and family I'd had and then proceeded to abuse me psychologically. I became their doormat until I ran away from home at fifteen. I managed over the years to pull myself together and vowed I would never depend on another. Ever." The whole time she had recited her brief past history, she kept her gaze trained on his face, gauging his reaction. Nothing but compassion entered his expression. But then she hadn't told him the worst part—she couldn't get those words past the lump crammed in her throat.

"You aren't telling me anything I haven't heard before. You can't shock me. I've seen so much as a child psychologist. But I will tell you, it's impossible to go through life relying on no one. We are social beings. We need people. We need to help and be helped. That's part of our basic makeup that the Lord gave us. You can run from it, but you can't escape that fact."

Thankfully the waiter chose that moment to serve them their salads, an assortment of lettuces accompanied by red peppers, cucumbers, black olives, feta cheese and grape tomatoes. Although she loved this kind of dish, her stomach constricted, making the thought of eating nauseating.

Shane speared his first bite with his fork. "You haven't said much lately about how Jason is doing. I'm hoping that means fine. I don't get a lot from Mrs. Bradley."

Because she didn't have much to do with Jason in class. "I mainly work with him and he is doing great."

"Any tantrums?"

"Less and less as I've figured out what to do with him, especially in new situations." Her stomach settled enough for her to sample her salad. "I won't kid you. He still doesn't like change and will get upset. I usually can head it off before it becomes a full-blown tantrum." She smiled. "But he's starting to interact with some of the students in his class. I even got him the other day to sit at the table and do some of his work there."

"Great. You're so good for my son."

The compliment caused a blush to move up her neck and all over her face. "He's special."

While they finished their salads, silence reigned, except for the low murmurs of the other diners and the soft strains of music in the background. Her tension began to flow from her as she let the peaceful surroundings seep into her.

The ring of her cell disturbed that tranquility.

"I've got to answer this. Sorry." She quickly dug into her black purse and retrieved her phone. When she saw the number on the display, she frowned. "Whitney here."

"Come get me," Amanda whispered, her voice laden with tears. "Hurry."

Chapter Eleven

"Is this the place?" Shane asked as he parked on the street outside a small house, one light shining from a front window, the drapes pulled.

"Yes, this is where Amanda told me she lived, but she's not outside waiting. Something's wrong." Whitney shoved open the SUV door and started to descend.

Shane grabbed her. "Don't. Let me go check."

On the ride here—over twenty *long* minutes—she had told him everything that had happened between her and Amanda over the past seven weeks and realized he had good reason to be concerned. She peered back at the worry in his eyes. "If you go alone and the boyfriend is there, he'll think she is seeing someone else. No telling what he'd do."

"He could harm you. Stay here." He released his grip and hurriedly opened his door.

The flush of anger radiated from her face. She squeezed her hands into fists and waited until Shane was a few feet from his car before exiting the SUV. The sound of the vehicle's door closing pivoted him around to face her. He stalked back to her.

"What about 'stay here' don't you understand?"

"I understand precisely what you want." She lifted her chin and narrowed her eyes although in the dark he probably didn't see the fury in her expression, mostly directed at Amanda's boyfriend. "You won't tell me what to do, Dr. McCoy. I'm coming with you. If Hayden is there, I'll do the talking. I know what these lowlife scumbags are like." She marched past him, quickening her steps the closer she came to the house.

While Shane came up behind her, she rang the bell then knocked when there wasn't an answer. Music blared from the back. Maybe no one could hear. But Amanda knew she was coming and was supposed to be outside. Why wasn't she? Fear replaced her anger as she went to the window and peeked through the slit in the drapes. Shane continued pressing the bell.

What little she could see suggested a struggle. A coffee table was upturned. Shards of glass littered the hardwood floor. Her fear skyrocketed.

She rushed back to the door. "There's been a fight. What I can see of the living room has been destroyed." Jerking open the screen door, she tried the knob. *Amanda's in trouble. Please, Lord, help me.*

It gave, swinging wide at Whitney's touch. She took a step inside.

Shane held her back. "At least let me go first."

The look he sent her commanded her cooperation. She nodded.

The small entrance flowed into the living area. Someone in a rage had plowed through the room, taking it apart. A chill flooded her when she saw a hole in the wall as though a fist had struck it. Bloody fingerprints scored the doorjamb leading into the kitchen.

Shane flipped his cell open to call 9-1-1 as he picked his way across the debris scattered everywhere. She dogged his steps, her stomach churning more with each one she took. Memories of her own situation that had driven her finally to seek the help that had saved her life swamped her. Shudder after shudder rippled down her length.

While Shane headed toward where the noise was coming from in the next room, in the kitchen Whitney saw two feet, barely visible, the rest of the body hidden by the counter. Her heart pounding, she rushed forward. "She's over here."

Amanda curled against the crook where the counter met the wall. The side of the young woman's face that Whitney could see was bloody and battered. Like the abuse a punching bag took. Her past rushed forward, whisking her back to another time. All she could see for a moment was the fist coming at her, over and over. All she could feel was the numbing fear and pain over every inch of her when she could no longer fight back.

That last time she'd thought he would finally kill her.

Shane laid a hand on Whitney's shoulder. Gasping, she flinched. "Is she alive?" Shane asked.

Whitney shook the memories away. Amanda needed her. "Amanda. It's Whitney." She touched her friend.

Amanda pressed herself farther into the corner. "No. No. Please leave me alone. I won't burn the pork chops again."

The woman's wails tore through Whitney as though she'd been ripped apart. "We need to get out of here. You're safe now."

"No. No, he'll be back."

"I'm not alone. I have my…" Whitney glanced over her shoulder at Shane and continued, "my friend here. C'mon." Gently grasping the young woman, Whitney tugged on her arm, trying to get Amanda to move.

Finally her co-worker peeked up at Whitney then Shane. Beneath Whitney's hand, Amanda's tension coursed. She shifted, unfolding her small frame while keeping her face turned away from Whitney.

A commotion at the front of the house, then her name being shouted, sent Amanda back into her cocoon of terror, her whimpering muted by her head buried against her shoulder.

"I'll go see what's happening. Meanwhile you get her out of the house by the back door," Shane whispered loud enough for both Whitney and Amanda to hear.

He straightened to his feet and started for the living room.

A large man, a few inches taller than Shane's six feet, barreled into the kitchen through the hallway entrance, a six pack of beer cradled in the crook of his arm, a bloody scratch across one cheek. Good. Amanda had at least fought back before being overpowered.

For a few seconds the brute froze with surprise, locking gazes with Shane, which gave Shane a chance to wheel around and place himself between the boyfriend and the woman. Teetering, the man tossed the beer on the counter nearby, the sound of it striking the tiled top jarring in the quiet. His face red with fury and too much liquor, Hayden fisted his hands at his sides while gauging Shane as an opponent.

Whitney covered Amanda with her body. From

the brief glimpse Whitney had seen before Amanda retreated again, there wasn't a place on her face that her boyfriend's fists hadn't hammered. She wouldn't let Hayden hit her friend one more time.

"Get out of my house!" the man shouted, his bloodshot eyes pinpoints.

"The police are on their way." Steel and ice threaded through Shane's voice.

The brute stumbled forward but had to grip the counter on the other side of the room to steady himself. Shane matched each of his moves, blocking any immediate access to Amanda. His presence seemed to magnify as he stood his ground, the table the only thing between him and the enraged, drunken boyfriend.

As the two men squared off, Whitney assessed Amanda and her chance of escaping with the woman. The back door was to the right, only three feet away. She turned and murmured into Amanda's ear, "We're leaving. If you don't now, he'll kill you. I've been there. I know what will happen." *Where are the police?*

The sound of a dish shattering against the floor stole Whitney's voice. She swallowed but nothing wet her parched throat. Her own cell was in her purse in Shane's SUV. She had no way of calling 9-1-1 again.

This time when she gripped Amanda, she conveyed the urgency in the situation. "C'mon. You can do this."

One swollen eye popped open and peered up at her. "Get out before…" Terror snatched the rest of Amanda's words as Hayden threw a chair at Shane.

Deflecting it with his arm, he dodged the full impact of the piece of furniture. It crashed against the counter a foot from Whitney.

"If I have to drag you out of here, I will. I won't let him get you," she said with such force, her message finally penetrating her friend's haze of fear that had held her immobile.

With her hand around Amanda's arm, Whitney started for the back door with the young woman right behind her.

"No!" Hayden screamed. "I won't let you leave me."

He slammed into Shane, taking him down to the floor. While he wrestled with the boyfriend, Shane muttered, "Get her out of here."

Whitney pulled Amanda through the door, then whirled around and said, "The police are on the way. You go out front and hide until they come."

"Where are you going?"

Whitney barely heard the mumbled question, especially with the racket coming from the kitchen. "I'm going to help Shane."

"Don't!" Panic infused Amanda with strength as she clutched Whitney's arm. "He'll kill you."

She wouldn't let that man hurt Shane. She had to try and help. If something happened to Shane, she'd never forgive herself. Whitney shook Amanda's grip off her. "Go. Now or all this will be for vain."

Her hand on the knob, Whitney tapped her foot against the back porch as she watched her friend hurry toward the side of the house. As soon as she disappeared, she'd try to get to the phone in the kitchen and call 9-1-1 again. She even envisioned using the receiver as a weapon against Hayden.

As Amanda rounded the corner, it became quiet on the other side of the door. A blanket of sweat drenched Whitney.

Please, Lord, let Shane be all right.

Her heartbeat thundered in her ears. Trembling, she thrust open the back door, preparing herself mentally to do battle to save Shane and Amanda. Hayden lay sprawled on the floor with Shane looming over him, his body rigid, anger slashing his face.

"What happened? Are you hurt?" Whitney wanted to go to him, feel his arms about her to help wipe from her mind the ugly scene that had just occurred, but she remained still near the door.

"I'd managed to get away from him when this

happened." Shane gestured toward the prone body. "I think he passed out." He knelt and felt for the man's pulse at the side of his neck. "He's alive."

"Let's tie him up, so if he comes to, he can't hurt anyone."

"Not a bad idea. See if you can find something. I want to stay here just in case he does come to."

She would like to do more to Hayden for all the pain he'd caused Amanda. At least she would have the satisfaction of removing his object of obsession from him, and she would use every ounce of her know-how to make sure Amanda stayed away from the man. Although while living in the woman's shelter in Houston, she'd seen more than one abused victim go back to her abuser, she wouldn't let it happen here.

She checked the drawers in the kitchen and didn't see anything so she moved toward the living area. The front door flew open, and two uniformed police officers with their weapons drawn filled the entrance. Relief trembled down her length. Help had finally arrived. At least Shane wasn't hurt and Amanda was alive. Clutching the back of the lounger, she sagged against it.

"The lady outside said her boyfriend was trying to kill someone," the male officer said, scanning the room.

"Shane has her boyfriend subdued in the

kitchen for the moment. He was drinking and passed out before he could do any harm to Shane. Where's Amanda?"

"Sitting in the patrol car until the ambulance arrives. She's been beat up bad." The man's female partner made her way toward the kitchen. "She could use a friend right now."

"I'll go check on her."

"That would be appreciated." The female officer disappeared into the kitchen.

Whitney hurried outside on the porch and down the sidewalk to the patrol car. When she opened the back door, she found Amanda again curled up on the seat, sobbing into the leather.

"Amanda, it's over. You're safe." She stooped into the vehicle, making sure her friend heard her. "The police have Hayden. They'll take him to jail. You'll get some medical help." Of course, that was only the beginning of the journey for Amanda, but she would help her every step of the way.

"I'm alone. I'm alone. He loved me."

Whitney got down as close to Amanda as she could maneuver in the tight space. "No, he didn't. People who love someone don't beat them. I don't care what he said. Actions speak louder than words." When her friend shifted so she looked at Whitney through swollen eyes, she continued, "Remember I've been in your shoes. I know exactly what you're going through. You are not alone. I will help you."

"And I will help you," Shane interjected, appearing at the car door, as an ambulance siren sounded a few blocks away. "I know an excellent counselor you can see at no cost."

For a few seconds Whitney drank in the unharmed sight of him, realizing what could have happened if he hadn't been with her when she'd come to pick up Amanda.

I couldn't have done this alone.

That implication rocked the foundation she'd erected for herself. If she'd tried to do this alone, she could have gotten Amanda killed—and possibly even herself. She shivered in the cool night.

"I can't accept that," her friend mumbled, her words slurred by her puffy, cut lips.

"Yes, you can. Accept the help, then when you can, help another woman in this kind of situation get out of it." Whitney assisted Amanda up.

The flashing red and blue lights on the ambulance sliced through the darkness as the vehicle careened around the corner at the end of the street and raced toward the patrol car. After the paramedics had checked out Amanda initially, they placed her on the stretcher and began to wheel her toward their vehicle.

"No, stop!" The young woman reached out

toward Whitney. "I can't go by myself. Please come with me."

Whitney glanced at the nearest EMT.

"Fine, you can ride in back with me."

Shane took her hand. "I'll follow you to the hospital as soon as I talk with the police. I'm going to make sure that man stays in jail even if Amanda doesn't press charges."

Words she hoped proved true, but sometimes the system didn't work. Somehow Amanda had to press charges. "I can get a ride to my place later if you need to go home."

He turned her toward him and cupped her face. "We're in this together. I'll call Aunt Louise and let her know what's going on. I'll be there as soon as I can." Shane walked with her to the ambulance and helped her up into the back. "Remember what you told Amanda tonight?"

She shook her head, not sure what he was referring to.

"You aren't alone. That goes for you, too." He leaned forward and brushed a quick kiss across her lips before striding toward the house.

Stunned, she watched Shane vanish inside. She still felt the soft touch of his mouth on hers as though he had left her branded.

"Ma'am? Ma'am, it's time for us to go." The paramedic gently jostled her arm to get her attention.

A blush heating her face, she turned into the ambulance and sat, wanting to deny the claim Shane had declared to the world. He was interested in pursuing a relationship with her. *What am I going to do about that?*

Shane parked out in front of his house and switched off his SUV engine. "C'mon. I'll walk you home."

Whitney shoved open the car door. "You don't have to. You have to be as tired as I am."

He rounded the front of his vehicle and took hold of her hand. "I don't think I can sleep after the night we've had."

"Yeah, but at least Amanda doesn't have any broken bones and is now comfortably settled at the McKinney Women's Shelter."

"And if Kelli McKinney has her way, Amanda will press charges against her boyfriend. Kelli is one determined woman."

"Amanda won't at first. She'll think of all the things she thinks she's done wrong to Hayden. But you're right. Kelli knows what to do." Whitney paused on the sidewalk in front of Zoey's house, the gray of predawn spreading over the landscape, an early morning chill still in the air. "I'm glad you talked Amanda into seeing the therapist you know. Hopefully between Kelli and the therapist, Amanda will do the right thing." If it hadn't been for the one who'd come to the shelter in Houston that Whitney had gone to, she might have continued the relationship that had put her in the hospital two times.

"It's still going to be a long road for your friend." He resumed walking toward her apartment. "But you already know that."

"Yes," she said on a long sigh, knowing that she and Shane needed to finish their conversation that had started at the restaurant the night before, especially after what he'd heard when she'd been talking to Amanda. "Want to come in for some coffee?" she asked as she mounted the stairs to her place. Shane was too good for someone with her past. He deserved someone like Becka. Which meant she needed to end this dating gig before she fell totally in love with him and really ended up hurt. But the pain in her heart made a mockery of her attempts at thinking she could go through life alone, not needing anyone.

"That sounds nice. Maybe yours will rid me of the taste of the hospital's vending-machine coffee."

She unlocked her door and tossed her purse on the nearby chair, then trudged to the kitchen and quickly put the caffeine-laden drink on to brew. As its aroma wafted through the apartment, Whitney washed her hands and face, and unlike

Shane, thought she could sleep for hours. Revisiting an emotional journey she'd already taken had drained her, and yet she knew she would have to continue on the journey because she'd decided no more secrets between her and Shane. If they were going to date, move their relationship to the next level—and she realized she wanted that after the past ten hours with a man who'd stood between Hayden and her—she needed to tell him *everything* about her past.

With two mugs, she sat across from Shane at the kitchen table. "After living on the streets for a while, I became involved with a guy five years older than me. I thought everything would be all right from that moment on. My real troubles were just beginning. He abused me, but what was so bad was that I let him. I thought he was right every time he accused me of not doing something correctly. But no matter what I did, it was never good enough. Someone helped me get out of that awful situation but it wasn't easy. My self-esteem was so wrapped up in him. We'd been together for three years. He was the one who got me off the streets. I had three meals and a roof over my head. I felt in his debt for that." She lifted her quivering hand with the mug in it and took a long sip of the hot brew. "So yes, I know what Amanda has gone through."

"This explains why you are so determined to do

everything on your own. But what that man did to you wasn't normal for a relationship. A true one is loving, a mutual partnership, each person equal."

"Is that what you had with Becka?"

Shane nodded.

"I haven't found that to be the rule."

He stabbed her with an intense, probing look. "You haven't been looking in the right places."

"Like Cimarron City?" She grinned and savored the strong flavor of her coffee. He wasn't heading for the door. He was still here talking to her as though she were important to him.

"I'm sure we have our share of good—and bad—guys like any town."

"And you just happen to be one of the good guys."

A flush spread across his face. He raised his mug to cover his expression partially as he took a drink.

"I did learn one thing tonight." She snagged his questioning look. "I could have been hurt or possibly killed if you hadn't been there to help. I couldn't have done this by myself."

"Then I'm glad I was there." He downed the last of his coffee.

Whitney stared down at the dark brown of her drink, trying to get enough courage to say the rest of what she needed to tell Shane. There was no way but just to tell him. With a heavy sigh, she looked into his face. "That's not all you need to know about me. The reason I took all that abuse from that man was I felt I deserved every blow."

"No one does."

"I realize that now, but at the time I was sixteen and didn't know." She averted her gaze. *Please give me the strength to finish what I started—Lord.* "I was homeless as a teen, and for a while I sold myself to survive. He knew that and never let me forget it." Visually she reconnected with Shane, preparing herself for the disdain in his expression. Instead she saw compassion and tenderness. Her heart swelled at the sight, filling her with a sensation of such love she was stunned by its power. She blinked, wondering if it was an illusion.

He rose and came to her, pulling her up into his arms. "Thank you for sharing that with me. It couldn't have been easy and I feel honored." He framed her face. "Is that why you don't feel worthy to have the Lord's love?"

Her throat closed, she simply nodded.

"'Though your sins be as scarlet, they shall be as white as snow.' That's from Isaiah and that's God's view on forgiveness. There is nothing—let me emphasize that, *nothing*—that the Lord will not forgive if you come to Him with repentance in your heart. All you have to do is ask Him for that forgiveness."

"That's too simple. How could He?"

"Jesus didn't care where a person had been, only where he was going. He died for our sins—not just certain ones, but *all* of them."

Tears sprang into her eyes and streamed down her cheeks.

"And I'm not going to do any less, either. That person you were isn't who you are today. You are a loving, caring woman who I care for very deeply." He ran his thumbs across her cheeks.

But her tears continued as though washing the last remnants of doubt from her soul. He drew her against him, and she cried. When there was nothing left inside her except a calmness and peace she'd never experienced, she leaned back and took his face within her hands.

"You're a special man. Thank you for being—my friend."

He smiled, a tender expression deep in his eyes. "Who wants to continue our interrupted date. How about next Saturday night we resume the one we were on last night?"

"The world's longest date?"

"Yep."

"Sure. It sounds like fun." Her pulse pounded at the thought of going out with him on what she would consider their first real one with everything out in the open between them. A new beginning.

He slid his fingers through her hair and held her

head still while he slanted his head and settled his mouth over hers. As his kiss deepened, marking its place in her heart, another phase in her life was starting—scary and one she wasn't sure she could do right but she was going to try.

He drew back. "I'd better be going. Give you a chance to get some sleep before church today. Jason has been looking forward to you attending his Sunday-school class all week as his guest helper."

"I'd forgotten with all that's been happening. That's today." Whitney checked her watch. "That's only three and a half hours away!" Two weeks before she had agreed to be Jason's guest because most of the children had their mothers to fill the role. After her initial panic, she'd been flattered he'd asked her.

She followed him to the door, her hand in his. Outside on the stoop she paused next to Shane who leaned against the railing staring up at the sky. Infused in the powder blue were all the bright hues from coral to mauve. A sun yellow fingered its way through the myriad ribbons of color.

"Beautiful," she whispered in the quiet of dawn.

"God must have had fun creating this world." Shane slipped his arm around her shoulder and turned her toward him.

"Yeah, but what a wonderful job He did."

Shane kissed the tip of her nose. "See you later."

She watched him leave, then stared again at the majestic display of colors in the sky unfolding before her. *I've done so much wrong in my life. Please forgive me.* She hung her head, wondering if this peace she felt would go away. It didn't.

Looking heavenward, she said, "Lord, I'm Yours to do as You want. Show me the way."

Chapter Twelve

After sharing a cup of coffee at a café, Amanda slipped into Whitney's car. "You saved my life, Whitney. Hayden would have killed me that night. I know that now. I'd have been dead if he hadn't gone out to get more beer."

"And you used that time to call me. You aren't dead. You have the rest of your life before you." Whitney pulled out into the traffic.

"Yeah, but I don't know what to do now. All I did for years was live from one day to the next. I feel so lost."

"What do you want to do?" *Good question, Whitney, for yourself. What do you want to do?* For so long she'd thought love wasn't a prospect for her, but now she was thinking just maybe the type of love Noah and Cara had was possible for her, too.

"Work with children. My job has shown me that at least."

"Do you want to be a teacher?" A few blocks from the café, Whitney drove down the alley next to the McKinney Women's Shelter.

Amanda shook her head. "I don't think I want that now. I do enjoy being with the children here at the shelter and school. I've helped some with their homework and played games with them, but I want to help women in trouble like you did for me."

She'd only done what someone had done for her. "You've got time. It took me years to finally decide I wanted to go back to school to be a teacher." Whitney idled her VW near the back entrance. "How's it going with the therapist?"

"She's wonderful. I've had several sessions with her in the past three weeks. Thank Dr. McCoy for me."

"Will do." Whitney instantly thought of the date she'd had with Shane just a few days before. They were spending a lot more time together—doing things as a couple, as well as including Jason in some of the activities. Being with Shane had opened her eyes to all kinds of possibilities, not just an everlasting love with him but the Lord, too.

"The one thing my therapist is teaching me is to be truthful to myself. For the longest time I kept thinking the next time Hayden wouldn't hit me, that he really meant he loved me but I'm beginning to see that wasn't so." Amanda pushed open her door. "Thanks for the ride. See you tomorrow. It'll be Friday. Any big plans for the weekend?" She grinned, a twinkle in her eyes. "With Dr. McCoy? I saw how he looked at you when he picked Jason up early from school today."

Heat scored Whitney's cheeks. "We're bike riding tomorrow evening if the rain holds off."

"You've got a good man there. Bye." Amanda hurried toward the back entrance into the shelter.

But am I the right woman for him?

As Whitney strolled down the driveway in front of her apartment, she put her hair up in a ponytail. She scanned the sky. Not a cloud could be seen. With the temperature in the low sixties, the weather was perfect for the bike ride. Although today at school had been a particularly long one with too many interruptions in Jason's routine, there would be no way she would miss this outing. It had been all the child had talked about in class—to the point that even Mrs. Bradley had called him down.

Heading toward Shane's house, she wished she had a solution concerning the teacher. Mrs. Bradley still wasn't interacting with Jason even though the children were more and more every day. Jason had his circle of friends who took care of him on the playground and at lunch. Today when Mrs. Bradley had told Shane's son to be quiet about the bike ride, at least she had sat next to him at the table and even looked at his work. So maybe that was a small step in the right direction.

As Whitney crossed the street, Jason and Shane came out of the house. Shane waved at her while he made his way toward his SUV in the driveway with one of the bikes to put in the back of his vehicle. He wanted to ride along the river path, which meant transporting the bikes to one of the parking areas along the trail.

His son followed him with his smaller bicycle with training wheels still on it. When he finally saw Whitney, Jason beamed, dropping hold of his bike on the sidewalk in front of the house. The child spun around and rushed to her. Laughing, she swung him around. His giggles filled the air.

"Hey, I could use some help here." Shane struggled to fit the other larger bike into the back of his SUV.

Whitney put Jason down and covered the short distance to Shane to see what she could do.

"I think I've got this one." Shane pushed in the one she used when they rode. "Bring me Jason's and let me see if it can go back here, too."

She walked toward Jason's bicycle. The blare

of loud music from a car radio and the screech of tires sounded. The child's attention riveted toward a red car swerving around the corner, only two houses away, then picking up speed on the residential street.

A big yellow Lab barked across the street in the front lawn. Jason turned his gaze to the animal and took a step toward the road then another. Then all of a sudden he darted forward out into the street.

"Jason, stop," she screamed, and started toward the child.

Jason didn't stop.

"Shane," she yelled, although she was closer to the boy by a good ten feet.

The horn blasted a continuous sound while the driver slammed on the brakes. Too little, too late. The car went into a sideways skid. Whitney increased her speed. Jason wasn't going to make it without getting hit. She dove the few remaining feet and shoved him out of the way of the careening vehicle.

The impact with the front bumper threw Whitney up into the air. When she landed on the hood, she slid and crashed to the pavement with a thump.

Shane paced the hallway outside the waiting room. He just couldn't sit and wait to hear how Whitney came through surgery to repair her shattered arm. The very thought of what she was—and would be—going through left him chilled to his bones.

"Here. It looks like you could use this." Noah thrust a coffee into Shane's hand.

"What if they can't stop the bleeding? What if…" Shane couldn't even finish his sentence, the implications wrenching his gut.

Whitney's brother paled. "The Lord's with her now. We have to rely on Him."

"The last time I relied on Him to take care of a loved one, she died." There was a part of him that was stunned he'd said that; another part, long buried, not even known to him, surfaced to taunt his declaration of having faith in God.

"If it's God's will, how can we argue with it?"

"I can." Shane stalked away, angry with himself for falling in love again, angry with the Lord for doing this to him again, and even angry at his son for running out in the street. "I've got to get out of here. Call me and let me know what happens with the surgery."

A moan escaped Whitney's lips as she shifted on the bed in the hospital room, trying to ease the pain that covered her whole body. But it continued to attack her although she was on pain medication. Up until a while ago she had been drifting in and out of consciousness. At least the grogginess was better, and she felt she could carry on a conversation now because there were things she wanted to know.

"Whitney, do you need me to get the nurse?" Her brother hovered over her bed, had ever since she'd awakened from the surgery several hours ago.

"I'm fine. Where's Shane?"

"He had to go to the police station to identify the teen driver. They caught the kid hiding at a friend's. He's on the way. It just took longer than he thought it would."

"The guy—didn't even stop?" She licked her dry lips and tried to reach for the water nearby, but she didn't have the energy to lift her arm.

Noah grabbed the cup and brought it to her mouth to drink. "No, hardly slowed down according to Shane, but he did get a good look at the young man."

"How's Jason, really?" She remembered pushing him out of the way, but something could have happened to him while the car fled the scene of the accident that they hadn't wanted her to know.

"I told you what Shane told me. He's okay. A few bruises and a skinned knee from hitting the pavement. That's all."

"And me? Are you telling me—everything?" The words came slow, as though her mouth had a hard time working right, but she was determined to find out everything.

Noah held up his hand. "I promise I am. You'll have to go through physical therapy to regain full use of your left arm. Your bruises and cuts will heal in time."

"How long recovering? I need to be—at work." Jason could fall apart without her. She was trying to get him to work with Amanda, but he wasn't there yet and Mrs. Bradley was out of the question. What would happen to Jason without her around?

"At the very least a week or so. Probably longer. Even then your arm will be in a cast. When that's removed, your physical therapy will start."

Her door swished opened and Shane appeared, his hair messy, a rumpled look about him, an unreadable expression on his face. His gaze connected with hers, and slowly some of the tension left his stance. He came farther into the room, standing at the end of her bed.

"How are you?" he asked in a formal voice.

"Not one of my better days." She attempted a smile to reassure him. The corners of her mouth quivered for a few seconds, and she gave up.

Noah glanced from her to Shane. "I think I'll leave you two alone."

"I'll sit with her. You take a break. Get something to eat. I saw Cara out in the parking lot leaving, and she said you haven't moved from Whitney's side the whole time."

Noah shook his head. "That's okay—"

Whitney closed her eyes for a few seconds, trying to fight off the last remnants of the anesthetic so she could find out how Shane was really doing. "You've been here all night. Go home, Noah. Get some sleep. The nurse is a button call away."

"I can't leave—"

"I'll feel like I need to entertain you. I don't think I'm up to being cheery and funny at this time. Maybe tomorrow."

Noah's mouth pinched into a frown. "I'll be back this afternoon."

After her brother left, Shane moved to sit in the chair near her bed. "You can drop the bravado front now."

Her shoulders sagged. "Great. I was getting tired." His eyes held a dullness to them. His straight posture as if he would break at any moment nibbled at her doubts. If she was truly going to be all right and his son was, then what was the problem? "How's Jason?"

"Fine," he bit out.

"Please don't blame him."

"I don't really blame him. I blame myself for

not teaching him before now about not running out in the street."

"Don't!" That word said with such force took part of what little energy she had. "You've been working with him."

"Obviously, I haven't been working hard enough."

Her eyelids slid closed again. "I've been trying to teach him, too, and haven't succeeded yet, either." One corner of her mouth tilted. "Obviously." Her gaze ran down the length of her. "What happened at the police station?"

"They've booked the seventeen-year-old for hit-and-run."

"I don't want him to do any jail time. I hope they treat him as a juvenile, not an adult."

"You sound like you want him to walk free. He needs to pay for what he did to you—could have done to my son. You don't speed down a residential street."

"If the Lord can forgive me, I can forgive him." Her eyes felt heavy and it took effort to keep them open.

"What if the next time he hits someone, he kills them? He needs to be held accountable for his actions."

"I agree, but not necessarily jail time." She yawned. "He has his whole life before him. He made a bad choice." She could remember some of hers as a teen.

Shane surged to his feet and began pacing.

Exhaustion cleaved to her. She didn't have the energy to fight this battle with Shane at the moment. Something was wrong, but she'd have to deal with it later. Another yawn escaped. Her eyes closed. The sound of Shane's footsteps became a rhythmic lure that quickly swept her into the darkness.

Shane stopped at the end of Whitney's bed and stared at her. Her bruises, scrapes and cuts stood out against the ashen cast to her face, taunting him with what had happened to her. Her arm, immobilized and bandaged, would be put in a cast for months. After it was removed, physical therapy would follow. A long haul. All because of him. If he'd never gotten himself involved with Whitney, she would be safe, not in pain and facing a long road to recovery.

Like Becka.

I can't do this, Lord. I can't go through this again. Not after Becka.

Shane collapsed into the chair by the bed to wait for Noah's return, then he needed to leave. Somehow he would be here for Whitney until she got back on her feet, but after that…

"Child, I want you to come to our house when you get out later today." Louise sank into the chair by Whitney's hospital bed and patted her hand.

"You need someone to look after you for a few days until you feel better."

"She's going home with me," Noah said from the small couch by the window.

Louise tossed him a glance. "Cara's got her hands full with the children. I can give her my un-divided attention."

"You've got Jason." Noah sat forward.

"Who is in school for part of the day."

"Hold it, you two. I think I have a say in where I go after I leave here. I'm going home." Whitney first looked at Louise then swung her gaze to her brother, aware of Shane standing silently behind his aunt.

Noah put his hands on his knees and pushed to his feet. "To my house."

Louise rose and glared at him. "I used to be a nurse. I know what to do."

"I can hire someone if I have to." Her brother moved toward Whitney on the other side of the bed.

She felt as if she were in the middle of a tug-of-war contest, but what really concerned her was Shane's silence since he'd arrived with his aunt. "I mean home to my apartment."

Next to the bed, Noah loomed over her. "You can't! You need to be taken care of."

Whitney's mind swirled with the argument and glares exchanged. "I may be momentarily incapacitated, but I will recover at my own place so this is not up for discussion. I still know how to take care of myself."

Her brother opened his mouth to say something.

"Don't, Noah. Aren't you supposed to be at work or something?" Whitney rubbed her hand along her temple. "I want to talk with Louise for a while. Alone." She fastened her gaze onto Shane. "I've seen both of you for the past two days. I need a change of scenery."

Shane nodded his acknowledgment and headed for the door. "I'll come back, Aunt Louise, in an hour to pick you up."

Noah leaned down and kissed Whitney's cheek, then followed Shane from the room, mumbling the whole way about how family should stick together.

Whitney released a long breath. "They both hover too much. I'm exhausted."

"I'm sorry for what just happened. I wanted to help. I made the situation worse."

The crestfallen expression on Louise's face caused Whitney to shake her head. She immediately regretted the action. The constant dull throbbing behind her eyes escalated. "No, don't feel that way. It meant a lot to me that you offered, but I think for everyone concerned I should stay at my apartment."

"You mean, Shane."

"You are a wise woman. What's going on with him? He's here in body but not in spirit."

"I won't kid you. Since the accident, he's withdrawn and hardly says a word to anyone, including Jason."

"How's Jason?"

"The usual. He doesn't understand what really happened. He's upset you aren't around, but trying to explain his role in it isn't sinking in. And every time Shane would say anything and get that blank look Jason sometimes gives, Shane would get frustrated and retreat further into silence. This reminds me of when…" The older woman snapped her mouth closed and shifted her gaze away.

"Reminds you of what?"

"When I first came to live with Shane and Jason, not long after Becka died," Louise said somberly, then pasted a smile on her face, but the look in her eyes reflected concern. "He just needs time. He could have lost his son that day and you. He's being reminded how fragile life is."

Was it that? Or something else? Has my past finally sunk in and he regrets dating me in the first place?

The phone rang, jostling Whitney from her thoughts. Since Noah had moved it closer to her the day before, she was able to reach for it and answer the call.

"Whitney, may I speak with my aunt?"

"Sure, Shane." She handed the receiver to Louise and tried not to eavesdrop on the conversation, but that was hard when the woman was sitting a foot away from her and the topic being discussed was Jason.

"Is everything okay?" Whitney asked when Louise hung up.

A frown carved deeper lines into her aging face. "Yes, it's not anything important."

"Don't try to protect me. What's wrong with Jason?"

Louise sighed. "Shane didn't want me to say anything to you."

"Something's happened at school." Whitney sat up a little straighter, clenching the bedsheet with her one good hand.

"Shane knows I'm not good at keeping quiet." She wagged her head. "He's going to school to pick up his son who has had a meltdown. That's the teacher's words, not mine."

A knock penetrated Whitney's haze of sleep. Lying on the couch in her apartment, she unfurled her body and struggled to her feet. Slowly she made her way toward the source of the noise, rubbing her eyes.

"Sorry about this, but Jason needed to see you," Shane said the second Whitney opened the door.

"No problem. Come in, you two." Whitney stepped to the side to let Shane and Jason inside, surprised that his son was with him during the middle of a school day. She was afraid to ask why. She knew Jason had missed a good part of Monday when Shane had picked him up because he'd had some problems. This was the first time she'd seen Shane since that morning in the hospital. She'd gotten her information second-hand from Louise.

Jason saw Calico and headed straight for the cat curled up on the windowsill in the living area. The child picked up the animal and laid her in his lap, then began stroking her.

Shane moved toward the kitchen, out of earshot of his son. "I tried to keep him away. He wanted to come yesterday right after you got home, but I wouldn't let him."

Why didn't you come see me? "He's always welcome here. So why isn't he in school?"

"He went this morning. There was another incident, but I can't get a straight answer from anyone at school, especially Mrs. Bradley. When I got there, Jason was in the reading corner, rocking back and forth, chattering to himself. It was lunch and he wouldn't get up."

She bit back the words "That was all?" and inhaled a deep, calming breath. "Did he throw a tantrum? Anything like that?"

"Monday he did, but today I don't think so. I'm getting the impression Mrs. Bradley doesn't know what to do with Jason."

Because she's chosen not to learn. Again Whitney kept her opinion to herself, but she had to bite the inside of her mouth. She needed to work on her patience.

"It makes me wonder what they would do if I refused to bring him home." Shane plunged his hand through his hair. "I've got an appointment tomorrow morning with the principal."

"Hopefully I'll be back sometime next week. I won't be totally up to speed, but I'll get the hang of doing things one-handed."

Shane frowned. "When you aren't there, they're going to have to come up with something that works. Jason staying home isn't an option anymore."

"Let me talk with him." Whitney hobbled to the couch, her body still bruised and battered but this was too important not to deal with now. "Hi, Jason. I hear you miss me."

He looked up at her while petting Calico. "Not at school."

"I will be next week."

"Miss you."

"I miss you. Tell you what. If you have a good day at school, when you come home, you can come over here and see me and Calico."

"Calico. Whitney." Jason dropped his head and brushed his hand along the cat's back.

Shane knelt in front of Jason. "Son, you have to stay at school all day to see Whitney. That means you need to do what Amanda says."

"Amanda," Jason repeated then returned his attention to Calico.

"Amanda is working with him?"

"I requested that today with Mrs. Bradley. She said yes. Amanda is at least familiar to Jason, not the sub they have for you."

"I agree that will be better than a stranger. I'll call Amanda tonight and talk with her about what works and doesn't work with Jason."

Shane straightened. "Jason has got to learn not to depend on just you at school."

Although she understood his reasoning behind that statement, Shane's words hurt. She couldn't help thinking that he was preparing to cut her out of their lives.

The two stayed for a half hour during which nothing of importance was discussed. Whitney felt as if she could almost see Shane building a wall between them with every minute they spent together. The energy to probe and delve deep into what was going on in his head evaded her.

"We need to go. But I'll be back later with dinner. Louise insists you at least let her fix you something for dinner."

Shane, with Jason in hand, was out the door before Whitney could tell him not to bring anything, that she had a refrigerator full of food from her brother and friends.

"It's so good to see you, Amanda." Whitney took up her seat on her couch as her friend sat across from her. "How did school go this week?"

"That's a loaded question, but let's just say Mrs. Bradley and myself will be glad when you're back next week. We've had a different person every day filling in for you. Will it be Monday?"

Whitney laughed at the eager expression on her co-worker's face. "Afraid not. I don't go back to the doctor until Tuesday. The earliest will be Wednesday. I thought Jason was doing a little better."

"He is. It's Mrs. Bradley. Anytime he does anything, she panics."

"He hasn't thrown another tantrum in the last few days, has he?"

"Nothing I can't handle, especially after you

told me what to do. And, honestly, I wouldn't call them tantrums. More like sit-down strikes."

Whitney smiled at the memory of that first week working with the child. "If he doesn't understand or hasn't been prepared, he'll do that."

"I've been doing pretty good, but Mrs. Bradley still springs stuff on us, me included. Just today—"

A knock interrupted Amanda.

"That'll be Jason and Shane. They've been coming over every afternoon as a reward."

Amanda rose. "Then I'll go. I just wanted to bring the cards by that the children made. Jason's is on top. I'll let them in so you stay seated. I want you well and back soon."

"Thanks, Amanda. Everything okay with you?"

"Kelli McKinney is helping me find an affordable place to live. Things are moving forward slowly. And I'm pressing charges against Hayden."

"That's great news."

Another knock echoed through the apartment.

"It sounds like someone wants to see you. Bye."

While Amanda let Shane and Jason into the apartment, Whitney picked up the top card on the pile from the table next to her. Jason drew a beautiful picture of him riding a horse. He hadn't gotten to ride in over a week and obviously missed it. So did she.

"This is a wonderful card, Jason. Thank you."

"Calico."

"She's on my bed. You can go find her." She held up the card Jason had drawn for her for Shane to see. "You should take him out to the refuge to ride. I'm sure Peter would work with him."

"I've already talked to Peter about Jason coming out after church on Sunday."

"Good," she murmured, feeling as though another activity she usually did with Jason was suddenly being taken away from her. It was irrational, but she couldn't shake the sensation she was being inched out of the child's life. "I hope I'm able to go to church and to the ranch by next weekend. I miss the children and the animals." *I miss you.*

Shane told her about Jason's past few days at school—at least the version Mrs. Bradley told him. "I've made it clear Jason will be a part of the class. His progress has been good. His therapist and I are pleased that he even managed to adjust in the first place. I know you're the reason he's made the adjustment so quickly."

But? She knew she wasn't going to like what he said next.

"Now we need to get him used to you not always being there for him."

She wasn't going to cry. This was good for Jason in the long run. No, she wouldn't always be around for him, and he needed to learn to function without her. But she couldn't stop the hurt from spreading.

Shane stood. "I'll be back over later with dinner."

"Yes, dinner," she mumbled, numb.

After gathering his son from the bedroom, Shane crossed to the door. Jason spied her on the couch and flew across the room.

The child threw his arms around her and planted a kiss on her cheek. "Miss you." He touched his chest. "In here."

Tears clogged her throat, and she choked out, "Same here."

Through the sheen she watched them leave her apartment. She closed her eyes, collapsed against the back cushion and prayed.

Not five minutes passed when another knock disrupted her quiet. Slowly she limped toward the door, checked through the peephole and tried to mask her surprise as she let Mrs. Bradley inside.

She must not have done a good job because her supervising teacher said, "I should have called but to be truthful this was a spur-of-the-moment decision on my way home from school."

"Have a seat," was all Whitney could say. Wariness took hold of her as she eased down on the couch.

"How are you doing?" Mrs. Bradley placed her

large leather brown purse in her lap and clutched the handles.

"I hope to be back at school Wednesday. A lot of my bruises and cuts will look better. I don't want the children to see me and get upset."

Her supervising teacher surveyed Whitney's injuries that were visible—mostly on her left side where she hit the pavement. "Yeah, I see what you mean."

Whitney gestured at her left cheek. "This is better than it was."

Mrs. Bradley dropped her gaze to her purse, her hand gliding across one of her straps. "I'm not sure where to begin."

Whitney shifted forward. "You didn't come to check on me?"

When the middle-aged woman reestablished eye contact with Whitney, doubt spread across her face. "I've been a teacher for twenty years, and I thought I was prepared for anything. I've dealt with children with special needs before when I worked at another elementary school in the district. I had a little boy in a wheelchair with a lot of medical problems. He would come into the room for an hour every day. I had another little girl with Down's syndrome, actually three children over the years. But none quite like Jason. We haven't had to handle them at Will Rogers Elementary until Jason."

Whitney flinched when Mrs. Bradley said "them" as though children with special needs were separate from other kids. *Lord, I need patience. I don't have a lot, at least when it comes to working with some adults.*

"As you know I fought against having Jason at Will Rogers. Now I realize even with what went on this week—"

"What happened this week?" She needed to understand what Mrs. Bradley thought the problem was.

"He's purposely defying me and others. When he was asked to do certain things by the teacher's assistant, he wouldn't. He'd sit down and not move. Even when I asked him. That first day you weren't there, he screamed and pounded on the table, floor and walls."

"When I first began working with Jason, I had to read up on autism. The one thing I discovered is how different each child with autism is. Jason is unique. Usually when he sits and won't move it is because he doesn't understand what's happening to him. He withdraws into himself. I don't even think half the time he's hearing what's being said to him. I have a book I can loan you if you would like. It helped me to understand some of Jason's uniqueness." *Please take it and read it.*

"I—I…" Mrs. Bradley gripped her purse straps

so hard that her knuckles whitened. "I may be too old for this, but the principal feels I'm the teacher who should have Jason. The other kindergarten teacher is fresh out of school and has a lot to handle as she begins her first year of teaching."

"I'll be glad to help you anyway I can. I want this to work for Jason, even when I'm not there." As she said the words, she realized she meant every word. If she was being inched out of the child's life because Shane was having second thoughts about her past, she still wanted Jason to do well wherever he was.

"I have discovered one thing this week. I need you to show me how to interact with Jason. I know you've been trying to get me to work with him, but I'll be frank with you. He's a challenge, and for a while, all I could think of was how inadequate I am with someone like him."

Thank You, God. It's a start. "I'll be glad to when I come back. Although I've talked with Amanda about Jason, I'd also like to train her more to work with him, too, in case I'm gone again." Whitney grinned. "Which I don't plan on."

"Done." Mrs. Bradley rose. "And I'd love to borrow your book. I can give it back to you by the time you come to school, hopefully on Wednesday."

The smile the woman gave Whitney warmed her heart. For the first time, she felt Jason had a chance at being really successful in kindergarten with everyone on his side. "I'll get it."

After Whitney retrieved it from her bookcase in her bedroom, she walked her supervising teacher to the door. "If you have any questions, feel free to call me. I'm starting to go stir-crazy confined to my apartment."

Mrs. Bradley chuckled. "I would have been two days ago. Thanks, Whitney, for your help. You will make a wonderful teacher one day."

"You know I'm going to night classes?"

"The principal shared it with me the other day. She wants me to help you learn while you're working with me." Mrs. Bradley tapped her temple. "She told me I had twenty years of experience to impart to you."

Whitney stood in the doorway as Mrs. Bradley descended the stairs, stunned at the offer to help her. *Okay, Lord, I've learned something today. Don't judge another. I know I'll have to have constant reminders. I'm a stubborn person and bad habits don't go gently away. I hope You're patient.*

With a sack in hand, Shane strolled up the driveway and stopped at Mrs. Bradley's car to speak with her. His gaze drifted to her once during the short conversation with Jason's teacher before he resumed his path to her apartment.

"When she told me she borrowed a book on

autism from you, I told her I had more literature if she wants to read anything else. She said she might and told me to tell Jason hello from her, that she'll see him Monday morning." Shane shook his head as he watched the woman back out of the driveway. "Amazing."

"Yes, that's what I'm thinking. After two months she wants to start learning how to work with Jason."

"That's wonderful." He held up the sack. "I brought dinner early." He studied her face. "It appears you've had no rest since Jason and I left."

"No, I'm fine. Come on in. I think we need to talk." She didn't want to wait for a bomb to fall. She would confront what she saw was happening the past week. Shane had been around physically but mentally he was somewhere else. She didn't want any regrets in their relationship.

Shane put the food in the kitchen, then came into the living area and took a seat across from her although there was plenty of room on the couch for him to sit.

"I understand that it's important for Jason not to depend on me at school and even other places like the refuge, but I hope that I can still be a part of his life. I've come to care for your son very much." *As I have you.* But she couldn't say those words nor could she come right out and ask him how he felt about her. *Are you having regrets about dating me?*

"You think I'm trying to push you out of my son's life?" His mouth pinched into a hard frown.

"No—well, yes, I do."

"Why would I do that? Jason responds to you better than he does most people. I wouldn't take that away from my son."

"Then tell me what's going on. You want Jason to work with others more and me less. When you are here, you keep your distance. I'm not very good at relationships, and I think I'm missing something here." All her frustration poured out in her words although she hadn't intended to broach the subject of Shane and her dating.

He rose to his feet at the same time he shoved his fingers through his hair, a sign he was clearly upset and frustrated. Not what she wanted to see. She'd hoped she'd been wrong about what she was feeling, that her imagination was working overtime to see something that wasn't there.

"I can't continue, Whitney. I thought I could, but this isn't working."

I will not cry. I will not cry. I knew this was coming. Love isn't for me. "I see. So that's the reason you want me out of Jason's life."

"No. No. I can't do that to Jason. I hope you'll

continue to work with him at school and at the refuge learning to ride, but…"

When he didn't continue, she said, "But you won't be around."

"I wish we could go back to being friends, but that's really not realistic. So yes, I won't be around much. I think that's best."

She made a choice as a teen—a bad choice—and she now had to live with the consequences. Although her heart was cracking open, she would—somehow—learn to go on without Shane. She'd actually started dreaming of what it would be like to have her own family, a husband and maybe even a child. Foolish dream.

She sank back against the couch, suddenly exhausted. All she wanted to do was sleep, for days. "I shouldn't have expected you to really forgive my past. That's asking more than most men could do." She cocked a grin that instantly faded. "Up until a few weeks ago, I hadn't been able to forgive myself. Thanks for telling me now rather than later." *One less day where I imagined I might have a future with you.* "Excuse me if I don't show you to the door. I've had a long day and I'm tired." She curled her feet up on the couch.

He crossed the few feet separating them and stood in front of her. "You think this is about your past!" Anger entered his expression. "When I told you I didn't hold anything against you, I wasn't lying to you."

"I didn't think you were at that moment. You've just had a change of heart. That can happen. It's a lot to truly take in."

"You were fifteen years old. A child."

"Still." She shrugged, desperate not to appear as though she were falling apart inside.

"It isn't your past. It's mine that keeps me from making a commitment. I'll never go through what I went through with Becka. There was a moment when I hit rock bottom and nearly did myself in rather than face life. I won't ever go there again."

All words fled her stunned mind. Before she could assimilate what he had said, he spun around and stalked to the front door. She flew off the couch, her body protesting the quick move. When she reached the stoop, however, Shane was nowhere in sight.

Chapter Thirteen

After bringing Jason home from school, Whitney followed him up to his house. Even though for the past two weeks she and Shane hadn't seen each other except from afar at church, the school or the refuge, she tried to spend some time with Louise and Jason when Shane was at work. But she didn't know how much longer she could do it. Being in his house, surrounded by his things, renewed the pain of his rejection each time she visited.

"I just put on a fresh pot of coffee. It looks like you could use some. A long week?" Louise ambled toward her favorite room, waving Whitney to take a seat.

"This was my first full week back at work since the accident and I'm dragging. I have so much homework from my college classes to catch up on, too. Thankfully my two professors were understanding and gave me some extra time. I'm not gonna get to spend as much time this weekend at the refuge like I want. My nose will be stuck in a big, fat textbook."

Louise put a mug down in front of Whitney, then took the chair across from her and sat. "Honey, you look like you're burning both ends of the candle. Excuse my cliché."

Whitney smiled then sipped at her warm coffee. "I'd excuse just about anything from you." She'd never had a mother, and Louise was becoming the closest thing to one for her—which probably wasn't a good development because of the strained relationship between Shane and her. No, strike that. There was no relationship between them.

Louise studied her coffee for a moment. "Then you won't mind me asking about what's going on between you and my nephew. I can't get him to talk about much of anything lately. He sulks around the house as though he's lost his best friend." She tilted her head to the side and examined Whitney closely. "And perhaps he has. Why aren't you two talking anymore? What happened?"

"What if I tell you nothing happened?"

"I wouldn't believe you."

Whitney lifted her shoulders in a shrug. "Honestly, I'm not really sure what happened."

"He never said anything to you?"

"Not exactly. He said something about we can't be together because of his past then stormed out of my apartment. I know how much he loved Becka. I guess he had regretted taking off his wedding ring and trying to move on." *Maybe he thinks my past doesn't bother him, but deep down it really does. I guess I should thank him for ending it now rather than later when my heart would be even more involved.*

"He told you that?"

"Well, no. But I didn't really understand what he meant by 'doing himself in.'"

Louise slid her hands slowly down her face. "When I first came to live with him, I suspected he had been contemplating taking his own life, but he never tried and he never said anything to me."

"Suicide? Shane?"

"He'd fallen apart after Becka and his unborn child were killed in the fire. He was overwhelmed with trying to care for Jason and pulling his shattered life together. The worse part is he didn't, at that time, have the Lord in his life so he was going it alone. I personally don't know how people who don't have faith can deal with tragedy like that without God behind them holding them up."

Would the Lord have given me strength to do something with my life sooner? I've made such mistakes and bad choices.

"My nephew's life was really rocking along. He was helping people right and left in a very successful practice. He had a son who hadn't shown the extent of his disability yet and a wonderful wife who was pregnant. Then his world fell apart. Almost everything was taken away from him—his possessions, even photographs, in the fire. His wife and unborn child gone in a flash." Louise snapped her fingers. "All except Jason, who soon after that began exhibiting more autistic traits. It was heartbreaking when I came to live with him."

"I'm so glad Shane had you. A lifesaver." Whitney leaned close to Louise. "Don't tell Noah, but I kinda look at my brother that way. My life wasn't going anywhere. I was going through the motions of living. That's all. Then one day my brother finally found me after being separated for twenty years. And he wouldn't let me go. He kept calling me until one day I decided to leave my dead-end job and life and start over."

Louise covered Whitney's hand. "The Lord usually works through others, and he did in your case."

First Noah and then Shane. Although Shane had pulled away from her, she would never forget how he had helped her change and brought her closer to the Lord. So who was going to help Shane now?

"I haven't wanted to pry, but you said you and

your brother were separated for twenty years. You had to be, what, eight or nine at the time. What happened? I know Noah stayed with the Hendersons for a while as a teen. Alice Henderson has mentioned how proud she is of her 'three boys' starting Stone's Refuge."

"Our father left us one day. Our mother had run away years before that. We were put into foster care. I was adopted while Noah wasn't."

"Oh, that's good." Louise sipped her coffee.

"No, not really. I would have been better off in foster care with my brother here in Cimarron City. My adopted parents weren't loving or accepting. In fact, I don't understand why they wanted me unless it was to do all the work around the house. I had a knack for going from one abusive situation to another." Bitterness laced with anger saturated her voice.

"You haven't forgiven your real or adopted parents. I can hear it in your words."

Whitney cocked her head. "What do you mean I haven't? Of course, I haven't! They beat me down in reality and figuratively. It has taken me years to put it behind me."

"And have you?"

"I try not to think about it."

"Is that working?"

Was it? Whitney inhaled a deep breath and held

it for a moment. "No. I've worn a chip on my shoulder for years because of my anger." Was this different from her wanting the Lord to forgive her?

"So they are continuing to control your life. What if you could be really free of the past? Would you do that?"

Whitney sat forward. "Yes! How?"

"By letting go of your anger and forgiving them for what they did to you. Once you do, they will no longer have any control over your life."

"It can't be that easy."

Louise frowned. "I never said it was easy. In fact, it is extremely hard at times. But, child, if you do, I guarantee you will be free to move on for the first time in your life."

The beautiful, serene smile that graced Louise's face touched a cord deep in Whitney and sparked the desire to be free finally of the yoke of her past. *But can I forgive both sets of parents? Can I forgive my boyfriend who abused me? Can I do what the Lord has done for me?* "How do I go about doing that?"

"Ask the Lord to help. He's there to guide you."

"I'm surprised dinner isn't ready," Shane said as he came into the kitchen and saw his aunt just beginning to pull the ingredients out of the refrigerator. "Did something happen?" Aunt Louise was a creature of routine and habit, like himself, which was good when dealing with his son.

"Whitney was here and we lost track of time talking."

The mention of Whitney always tightened a band about his chest. He missed her so much, but if he didn't make a clean break from her, he would never heal. But truth be told, there really wasn't any way he could totally be free of her unless he moved away from Cimarron City. Jason and even Louise were constant reminders of Whitney. And he couldn't find it in his heart to deny his son access to Whitney while she was nearby.

Suddenly Louise huffed then began stuffing the food back into the refrigerator. "I think we'll call in for pizza. Jason will like that, and I don't feel like cooking tonight."

Alarmed, Shane moved to her. "Are you all right? Did you have a TIA today?"

Her hand flitted in the air. "No, not that I know of. But you and I need to talk, and this is as good a time as any. Jason's still out back with Doggie." She gestured toward the table before the bay window. "We can keep an eye on him and talk at the same time."

He studied her for a long moment and saw that determined gleam in her eyes. It didn't bode well for him. "Aunt Louise, it's been a long day. Let's postpone it to another time."

She placed her fist on her waist. "Which means postpone it forever. No! Sit. Now."

Resigned to having this conversation with his aunt, he trudged to the table and plopped into a chair. And waited.

When his aunt sat, she checked on Jason out the window, then swept her sharp gaze to Shane. "Why have you hurt Whitney so much? All she's done for this family is help us. Look at what she did a few weeks ago. She saved your son's life."

He sucked in a breath. "You don't pull any punches, do you?"

"No, sirree."

"I can't go through a situation like what happened to Becka again. It's that simple."

"It's never that simple. There's something you're not telling me." She pinned him beneath her assessing survey.

She could make him squirm with that look. "Becka's dead because of me. Is that clear enough for you?" He lashed out in anger that sprang from a hidden source deep in him. "That man who set fire to my house destroyed my life."

"No, he didn't. You are, if you give him that kind of power. Have you forgiven him? Have you done what Christ did for us?"

He blinked, hearing her words but not believing them. "You want me to forgive him for killing Becka and my daughter? He murdered them."

"Yes, he was a sick man. It's the only way you'll be totally free. He and his actions after all this time still control you. Forgiveness will cleanse you of the past."

"How can I when I can't even forgive myself?"

"Ask the Lord for help. He will give it to you gladly."

"That man was one of my patients. I should have seen how desperate he was and been able to prevent what happened."

Louise's forehead wrinkled, her eyes narrowed. "Is that what you've been thinking all these years?"

Shane shot to his feet, his arms stiff at his sides. "Yes."

"You can't predict the future. You can't control the actions of others. Did he tell you what he was going to do?"

"Well, of course not."

"Did he indicate he was going to torch something?"

Shane shook his head, wanting to escape and relive that pain by himself.

"Then short of being able to read his mind, I'm not sure you could have stopped him."

"But he was troubled, despondent."

"I'm not surprised by that. He was coming to see a counselor. People who are happy and doing all right don't do that."

He spun on his heel and started across the kitchen. "I'm going for a walk."

"Shane, when you're able to forgive the man who killed Becka, you'll be able to forgive yourself. Think on that."

He emerged from his house and immediately looked toward Zoey's—as he had done every day since Whitney moved onto his street. He hadn't been able to break himself of the habit although he had been determined to wash her from his life.

Let's face it. It isn't working, McCoy.

So what am I going to do about it?

He strode down the sidewalk and headed away from Whitney's apartment and toward the park several blocks away. Emptying his mind, he basked in the glory all around him and desperately tried to find some kind of peace. By the time he arrived at the park, frustration gripped him and knotted his stomach. Peace eluded him.

After he found a bench in an area where there were no other people, he sank down on its wooden slats and settled his elbows on his thighs. Lacing his fingers together as though he were praying, he stared at the ground near his feet.

Father, I can't do this without You. I need help.

*How do I forgive the man who robbed me of my wife
and child? How do I forgive myself for not seeing
his troubled soul in time? How can I give Whitney
what she deserved when I'm afraid I'd lose her like
Becka and not be able to pull my life together?*

After talking with Louise, Whitney went back
to her apartment and picked up her Bible. She
read the Lord's Prayer in Matthew again and
again. Slowly the words sank into her mind. *If I
want God to forgive me, I need to be willing to
forgive others—all the others, not just the ones I
choose to. That includes my parents, the couple
who adopted me and my abusive ex-boyfriend.*

Can I do that?

Do I want my past to keep me trapped in anger?

No!

But again she felt the blows that struck her body
all those years ago. Over and over. She shuddered
with the memory. But those memories molded
her into a person who could help others who were
going through what she'd experienced. Like
Amanda. If she hadn't stepped in when she had,
her friend could have been killed that night.

Yes, but remember all those years—

"No, you won't win. I'm free of you. You can't
hurt me anymore. I forgive you. All of you. I
won't forget, but I'll forgive you." As she said

those words out loud, the shackles that had kept her bound to her past fell away. Free! The feeling exhilarated her.

She bowed her head and offered the Lord thanks.

Now she knew what she needed to do. She needed to help Shane do the same concerning his past. She no longer would stay away from him. Even if they didn't date, she would be his friend and help him to see how living in the past robbed him of the present.

Placing her Bible on the coffee table, she rose and strode toward her door. Out on the stoop she saw Shane jogging down the driveway toward her. His lines of weariness and hurt she'd seen the last time she was with him had vanished. He looked up at her and smiled, one that reached deep into his eyes and lit up his whole face.

He took the steps two at a time. "I jogged from the park. I'd like to talk with you. Okay?"

"What's going on?" Hope flared inside, but she tried not to let it have free rein.

"I've been so wrong about a lot of things. I want to explain and rectify some of my lousy choices, especially lately. One being, walking away from you." He tugged her into her apartment and shut the door, then drew her into his arms. "I didn't want the whole world to see this."

He feathered his lips over her, sending tingling

sensations spreading throughout her. Running his hands through her loose hair, he held her head still while he finally settled his mouth over hers and deepened the kiss until Whitney felt she was riding a Tilt-A-Whirl.

When he pulled back, still keeping her within the loose band of his embrace, she tried to assimilate what had just transpired. "What's changed?"

"Me." Taking her hand, he drew her toward the couch. "Let me start at the beginning. I had a patient, George, whom I had worked with several months. We weren't getting very far. He was a troubled young man who resisted counseling and was only there because his wife was going to leave him if he didn't. I thought we were making a little leeway, but certainly not what I'd wanted. George is the one who set fire to my house, which ultimately killed Becka and my daughter. He was trying to get back at me because I suggested he seek more intensive help at the Radar Psychiatric Clinic and Hospital."

Still clasping his hand, Whitney felt his tremors as he talked about the fire and George. She angled herself on the couch so that she could grasp both of his hands, conveying her support through her presence and touch.

"I hadn't seen the full extent of his problem, and for years, I've blamed myself for my wife's death."

His gaze linked with hers, an intensity of purpose in his expression. "But today I finally let my anger toward George go. I have too much to focus on in the here and now to stay in the past."

"Did Louise talk to you, too?"

His eyes widened. "Yes."

"She and I talked about forgiving the people who hurt me in my past. I have. My, she has been busy doing God's work today."

"That's my aunt for you." Shane grinned. "Also this good, hard look at myself has made me realize that I'm not in control. The Lord is. I have to trust Him to know what's best." He leaned back and pulled her against him. "When I saw the car hit you because you were protecting my child, all I could think about was being involved with me has put you in harm's way. I didn't want that again. I thought I couldn't deal with that guilt on top of the guilt I felt over Becka."

"You thought if you weren't around, I would be safe?"

"I was afraid to risk my heart again. The problem with that was you already had my heart totally. I've discovered that over the past few weeks. I know I can't live without you. I love you, Whitney Maxwell."

"I love you," Whitney said for the first time in her life.

She started to kiss him, but he held her back. "I want to marry you. Will you be my wife?"

She threw her arm around his neck, wishing she wasn't wearing a cast so she could really embrace Shane wholeheartedly. Then she kissed him. "Yes! How can I say no to a second chance at a family?"

Epilogue

"Jason, it's your turn to get your diploma." Shane prodded his son forward toward Mrs. Bradley.

Slowly Jason trudged down the aisle toward his teacher standing on the steps of the gazebo in the park. The audience of parents and friends of the kindergarten class erupted into applause as his son took his diploma and received a hug from Mrs. Bradley who smiled from ear to ear.

"I still can't believe they have a graduation ceremony from kindergarten," Shane whispered to Whitney.

"It marks the beginning of their life as an elementary school student. Did I tell you Mrs. Bradley is handpicking the perfect teacher for Jason next year?"

"No."

"Yeah, she's Jason's champion at the school

which makes me feel better about not being a teacher's assistant next year."

"But with your college classes, volunteering and the baby coming, you're going to have your hands full."

Jason approached them, removing the red—his new favorite color—ribbon around his diploma. When he peered up at Whitney, he thrust the ribbon into her hands. "For baby sister."

Tears misted Whitney's eyes. "She'll love it." She drew Jason against her and kissed the top of his head.

His wife felt Jason and he were her second chance at a family, but she was the one who gave him a second chance.

* * * * *

Dear Readers,

Both Whitney and Shane had people in the past they needed to forgive in order to have a life together. Forgiveness can be hard to do when someone did something awful to you. But anger holds people a prisoner to their emotions. The Bible has a lot of scripture devoted to forgiveness. It's in the Lord's Prayer. It is an important part of Christianity.

I love hearing from readers. You can contact me at margaretdaley@gmail.com or at P.O. Box 2074, Tulsa, OK 74101. You can also learn more about my books at:

http://www.margaretdaley.com.

I have a quarterly newsletter that you can sign up for on my Web site or you can enter my monthly drawings by signing my guest book on the Web site.

May God be with you,

Margaret Daley

QUESTIONS FOR DISCUSSION

1. Jason was autistic. Have you dealt with a child who has special needs? What has worked for you? What doesn't work?

2. Whitney thought that her sins were too much for the Lord's forgiveness. Do you think there is a sin so bad that the Lord turns away a person who truly repents? Why do you feel that way?

3. Whitney did some things when she was desperate that she regretted. Have you or someone you know done that? What happened? Were there any consequences to what you did?

4. Whitney loved to help people. What are some things you do to help others? Why do you like to do them?

5. Shane held himself back from Whitney because of his guilt over his wife. Has guilt ever stopped you from doing something you wanted to do? What happened?

6. What is your favorite scene and why?

7. Whitney thought she didn't need anyone. She could do everything herself. Can we really

live that way? Why or why not? How does God fit into this?

8. Forgiveness is the theme of *Second Chance Family,* not just God's forgiveness but forgiving other people. Do you need to forgive someone who wronged you? What did that person do? Can you forgive him? Why or why not?

9. Who is your favorite character and why?

10. Shane didn't want to have anything to do with being a rodeo clown, but for his son, he did it. What have you done that you didn't want to for a loved one?

11. Using animals to help children heal emotionally has been an ongoing part of the stories in the Fostered by Love series. Do you have a pet? If so, how does your pet make you feel?

12. Whitney never thought love was an option for her because of her past. What were some of the things that happened to her to change her mind? How did God have a hand in helping her to see the value to Him and others?

Dumped via certified letter days before her wedding, Haley Scott sees her dreams of happily ever after crushed. But could it turn out to be the best thing that's ever happened to her?

Turn the page for a sneak preview of
AN UNEXPECTED MATCH
by Dana Corbit, book 1 in the new
WEDDING BELLS BLESSINGS *trilogy,*
available beginning August 2009
from Love Inspired®.

"Is there a Haley Scott here?"

Haley glanced through the storm door at the package carrier before opening the latch and letting in some of the frigid March wind.

"That's me, but not for long."

The blank stare the man gave her as he stood on the porch of her mother's new house only made Haley smile. In fifty-one hours and twenty-nine minutes, her name would be changing. Her life, as well, but she couldn't allow herself to think about that now.

She wouldn't attribute her sudden shiver to anything but the cold, either. Not with a bridal fitting to endure, embossed napkins to pick up and a caterer to call. Too many details, too little time and certainly no time for her to entertain her silly cold feet.

"Then this is for you."

Practiced at this procedure after two days back in her Markston, Indiana, hometown, Haley reached out both arms to accept a bridal gift, but the carrier turned and deposited an overnight letter package in just one of her hands. Haley stared down at the Michigan return address of her fiancé, Tom Jeffries.

"Strange way to send a wedding present," she murmured.

The man grunted and shoved an electronic signature device at her, waiting until she scrawled her name.

As soon as she closed the door, Haley returned to the living room and yanked the tab on the paperboard. From it, she withdrew a single sheet of folded notebook paper.

Something inside her suggested that she should sit down to read it, so she lowered herself into a floral side chair. Hesitating, she glanced at the far wall where wedding gifts in pastel-colored paper were stacked, then she unfolded the note. Her stomach tightened as she read each handwritten word.

"Best? He signed it *best?"* Her voice cracked as the paper fluttered to the floor. She was sure she

should be sobbing or collapsing in a heap, but she felt only numb as she stared down at the offending piece of paper.

The letter that had changed everything.

"Best what?" Trina Scott asked as she padded into the room with fuzzy striped socks on her feet. "Sweetie?"

Haley lifted her gaze to meet her mother's and could see concern etched between her carefully tweezed brows.

"What's the matter?" Trina shot a glance toward the foyer, her chin-length brown hair swinging past her ear as she did it. "Did I just hear someone at the door?"

Haley tilted her head to indicate the sheet of paper on the floor. "It's from Tom. He called off the wedding."

"What? Why?" Trina began, but then brushed her hand through the air twice as if to erase the question. "That's not the most important thing right now, is it?"

Haley stared at her mother. A little pity wouldn't have been out of place here. Instead of offering any, Trina snapped up the letter and began to read. When she finished, she sat on the cream-colored sofa opposite Haley's chair.

"I don't approve of his methods." She shook the

letter to emphasize her point. "And I always thought the boy didn't have enough good sense to come out of the rain, but I have to agree with him on this one. You two aren't right for each other."

Haley couldn't believe her ears. Okay, Tom wouldn't have been the partner Trina Scott would have chosen for her youngest daughter if Trina's grand matchmaking scheme hadn't gone belly-up. Still, Haley hadn't realized how strongly her mother disapproved of her choice.

"No sense being upset about my opinion now," Trina told her. "I kept praying that you'd make the right decision, but I guess Tom made it for you. Now we have to get busy. There are a lot of calls to make. I'll call Amy." Trina dug the cell phone from her purse and hit one of the speed-dial numbers.

Haley winced. In any situation, it shouldn't have surprised her that her mother's first reaction was to phone her best friend, but Trina had more than knee-jerk reasons to make this call. Not only had Amy Warren been asked to join them downtown this afternoon for Haley's final bridal fitting, but she also was scheduled to make the wedding cake at her bakery, Amy's Elite Treats.

Haley asked herself again why she'd agreed to plan the wedding in her hometown. Now her humiliation would double as she shared it with family friends. One in particular.

"May I speak to Amy?" Trina began as someone answered the line. "Oh, Matthew, is that you?" *That's the one.* Haley squeezed her eyes shut.

* * * * *

*Will her former crush be the one to
mend Haley's broken heart?
Find out in
AN UNEXPECTED MATCH,
available in August 2009
only from Love Inspired®.*

Love Inspired SUSPENSE

RIVETING INSPIRATIONAL ROMANCE

These contemporary tales
of intrigue and romance
feature Christian characters
facing challenges to their faith...
and their lives!

**Four new Love Inspired Suspense titles are
available every month wherever books are
sold, including most bookstores, supermarkets,
drug stores and discount stores.**

Steeple
Hill®

Visit:
www.steeplehillbooks.com